Career Planning
after 10th and 12th

A teen's guide to Career Planning

Savita Marathe

VISHWAPRESS

Career planning after 10th and 12th
A teen's guide to Career Planning

First Edition: May 2016
© Author

ISBN - 978-93-85665-22-6

Disclaimer:
The information provided in this book is designed to provide helpful information on the topics discussed. The author and publisher have made every effort to ensure that the information in this book was correct at the time of printing. The author and publisher advise readers to collect all necessary information and make an informed decision. The names of institutions and websites provided in the book are solely for informational purpose only and do not constitute endorsement of any information provided by these websites. The information and links are subject to change, expire or be redirected without any notice.

Published by:
Vishwapress
An imprint of Vishwakarma Publications,
283, Budhwar Peth, Near City Post, Pune - 411 002.
Phone No: 020 20261157
Email: info@vpindia.co.in / Website: www.vpindia.co.in

Cover Design: **Meghnad Deodhar, Vishwapress**

Typeset & Layout: **Chaitali Nachnekar**

For those who are

"En Route"

to their career path.........

.

Table of Contents

Preface

Today's world offers a wide range of career options, hence determining what to choose comes a significant challenge. For the adolescents and young adults, especially those appearing for their 10th and 12th standard examinations, the priority decision is what they will study and how they will prepare themselves to build a successful career.

Generally these students and their parents start exploring various options though various sources like peer groups, teachers, experts or relatives and acquaintances but very rarely receive a non-judgmental and holistic opinion, which puts them in further confusion. As a career advisor I have come across many such students and their parents.

Although a lot of information is available in books, articles, on the internet, there is a need of a one-stop source of information about the different streams in 11th standard, subjects in each stream, entrance tests, eligibility, institutes etc. One also needs to understand which subject/s may lead to which career path/s to facilitate decision making and appropriate planning can be done.

"Career planning after 10th and 12th", is specially written with this purpose. The first part of the book gives an overview of the different stream and the subjects they contain, that a student can choose in 11th standard. Overseas education is gaining attention in our country, understanding this there is a chapter on IB Diploma program which can be chosen after 10th standard examination.

The second part of the book gives information about the various career paths arising from different streams, entrance examinations, eligibility requirements, likely career avenues etc. Students appearing for the 10th and 12th examinations sometimes get confused while choosing between career paths that are closely related which appear similar but have certain differences. I have tried to explain such differences in the related areas for e.g. Art and Design with an idea to help the student understand what s/he would actually like to do.

The last part gives some tips on how to plan the future education, the importance of planning and some tips on how to select a career path. The book contains many tables and flowcharts that will provide a visual imagery to explain things very quickly. At the end a bibliography of all important governing bodies, institutions and test conducting institutes is given. In short this book will serve as a ready reckoner for all those who are planning their education towards building a career path.

"Learning gives creativity, creativity leads to thinking, thinking provides knowledge, knowledge makes you great"

Book Reviews

In today's globalized world, career opportunities to students are immense. In earlier days, with fewer job opportunities, options of study ranged from Arts, Commerce and Science. Joining a Science stream proved one's intelligence because one could opt to become an engineer or doctor. You would study Arts to become a teacher and join the commerce stream to become a Banker.

However, presently there are several opportunities for students. Courses ranging from law, design, Management, economics, health sciences etc. Students are lucky because they can even switch from one career to the other, if they do interdisciplinary courses. However, such wide options also make students and especially parents confused. Therefore, what is needed for students is career guidance.

Ms. Savita Marathe has authored an excellent book on career guidance. She has given details of a wide range of careers, how to choose them, what is the eligibility criteria and what it would lead to.

This book is well timed and is the need of the hour. I am sure students and parents will be benefitted by reading this book

With regards,

Dr. Vidya Yeravdekar
Principal Director, Symbiosis
Member, Governing Board -
Indian Council for Cultural Relations (ICCR)
Former Member, University Grants Commission (UGC) and
Central Advisory Board of Education (CABE), Govt. of India

"En Route Career advisor" is a welcome initiative by Savita Marathe which has played immense role in shaping many careers. 21st Century brings several career options and one needs to seek expert opinion instead of following herd mentality. Know your strengths and focus on higher education leveraging that strength.

P+P = E is the new success equation.

Passion + Profession = Excellence.

If you know where your passion lies and make that as your profession then excellence automatically emerges. Can u imagine Sachin Tendulkar pursuing career as Java programmer in an IT company?

I heartily congratulate Savita for writing maiden book for advising young aspirants on global education and career opportunities. I am sure many editions of this book will be sold in near future.

Dr. Deepak Shikarpur
IT Entrepreneur, Author and Chairman Computer Literacy Committee Mahratta Chamber of Commerce Industries and Agriculture Member Academic council (Yashwantrao Chavan Maharashtra Open University)

This book will serve as a pathfinder for those who want to choose a right career. The author has taken a lot of efforts to overcome different aspects and difficulties one faces while choosing his/her career. This book is an eye opener for students as well as parents. The book has a holistic approach and is a valuable gift.

Dr. Makarand Thombare
Psychological Counselor,
Psychotherapist and Holistic Life Coach.

Acknowledgements

I would like to take this opportunity to thank my biggest support, my parents, Dr. Shivadeo and Mrs. Shailaja Bapat, who have supported me unconditionally all through my life. I also wish to thank my daughters Shweta and Shruti and son in law Ajinkya for their support. A special mention of Sanika, my niece for her valuable inputs in the book.

I would also like to thank Dr. Shriram Geet, a senior Career Counselor, for teaching me the technique of analysing the aptitude test report and mapping it with the student's interests. Special thanks to Ms. Mrunal Belwalkar, a freelance editor for editing the book and Ms. Meghna Majethiya for her inputs in the book title and cover design. Special credit to Dr. Deepak Shikarpur for his motivation, without which this book wouldn't have happened. I also take this opportunity to thank Vishwakarma Publishers for publishing the book.

I hope this book is helpful to all those who are going to put their first step on the career development path and wish them a bright and successful future.

All the best!!

Savita Marathe

Foreword

The book "Career Planning after 10th and 12th – a teens guide to choose the right path", is an admirable attempt. Written specially, for the students from 10th standard to 12th standard, this book helps as a guide for both, the students and their parents as it deals with the available career opportunities - conventional as well as nonconventional. It also talks about the role of an aptitude test in the career planning process.

Career development is a long-term process and requires meticulous planning at different stages. The initial stage of this process begins right at the 10th and 12th standard, where the student has to select a stream. However, at this stage, the students are still quite naïve (in knowledge about the outer world as well as experience). Selection of the stream is the first step of the career planning process that needs to be done very carefully. The wide variety of the available career options puts the students and their parents further in the state of confusion. At this point, what is more important for the students is to understand their interests, abilities, capacities and to discuss it with their parents. This will facilitate the decision making process. It's the responsibility of the parents to understand what their child is interested in and is good at, and appropriately guide and support him/her in choosing a right career path. This book is a commendable effort by the author in this direction.

This book gives an overview of the different streams available after 10th standard, including the subjects offered in each stream. It also gives details of the different career paths that arise from these streams, various entrance tests and their eligibility criteria. In other words, it gives options to parents as well as students, which will help them choose a stream and subjects accordingly in the 11th standard. This is supported by a detailed study of institutions in respective fields. Additionally, the website links given in the book will be helpful for those who wish to ascertain the details of the institutes.

Students, sometimes, may not have a clear idea about a particular career, for e.g. one may not have a clear idea about what is art and design. S/he may not be able to figure out whether there is any difference between a career in art and design, psychology and psychiatry or computer science and IT, which will make things difficult for them. These points are explained in such a manner that a layman can easily understand. This I think is excellent, as it will help the students in a big way in deciding their career paths and choose a stream accordingly. The chapter on Aptitude Test, which discusses the importance of the aptitude test in understanding one's abilities and how it helps in selecting a career path, is well explained.

Furthermore, the use of charts, tables, and bullet point text makes the book easy to read. At the end, the author has explained the importance of skills like planning, goal setting, time management etc. which, I feel will be useful to the students for their lifetime.

I feel, it is the need of the hour but very few such books are available. I congratulate the author for her efforts in compiling this useful information and offering it as a complete package...

Prof Dr Arun Jamkar,

MS. Ph.D. (Surgical Oncology), FICS, FIAGES, FMAS, FAIMER Fellow, Consultant, Persistent system Pvt. Ltd, Ex Vice Chancellor, Maharashtra University of Health Sciences, Chair National Bioethics Curriculum Implementation UNESCO Chair in Bioethics Haifa, Ex Dean, B J Medical College Pune and RCSM Govt. Medical College Kolhapur, Ex Professor of Surgery B J Medical College Pune.

Introduction

Rahul, a 24-year-old intelligent young boy, came to me recently for career guidance. Rahul had acquired a Bachelor's Degree in Civil Engineering from a reputed college in Pune. He had failed in one subject in the first year of engineering but because of the *'allowed to keep term'* or *'ATKT'* system, he didn't lose a year. Being a sincere student, he subsequently cleared the subject in the following year, and managed to complete the four year course with an overall second class.

Even though he is now a civil engineer, Rahul does not wish to work in that field because he doesn't like it. The reason he opted to get an engineer's degree in the first place was because his parents wanted him to. At the time, civil engineering was considered 'a hot market'. Additionally, Rahul himself was confused and didn't know what to do; so he went along with his parents' decision. After spending more time talking to him, I realised that he was a creative person; his mind was full of innovative ideas. He had also helped many of his architect friends creating 3D visuals for their designs. He could have become a good product designer, or even an architect had he known better. Subsequently, Rahul's aptitude test report also indicated that he had excellent potential to become a designer. If Rahul had spoken to his parents openly about his confusion, Pune could have witnessed the birth of a creative and innovative designer. On realising what had happened, Rahul also expressed his concerns regarding his younger brother, who was then studying in the 9th standard; Rahul didn't want him to make the same mistake that he did.

1

As a career advisor I come across many such examples. One wrong choice makes the students unhappy and the "Struggle Phase", which should ideally start at the beginning of the chosen occupation, starts in the 11th standard itself. This might continue until their formal education is complete or sometimes throughout their life. This struggle continuously goes on in the student's mind because they are doing something, which they don't like and thus don't find interesting. The first and foremost indicator of such phase is a drastic drop in the 11th and 12th standard marks which may continue in the subsequent studies also affecting their education and future career goals. This often leads to anxiety, confusion, and restlessness, as the students are not doing what they are really good at, what they really wish to do, or what interests them the most. At the same time, these late-adolescents, young adults are also passing through many physiological and psychological changes, which make them more vulnerable. The smallest, seemingly most insignificant of incidents can take a serious emotional toll, and may induce depression.

Thus, the selection of proper 'stream' after passing the 10th standard and 12th standard examination is a very important and crucial decision to take. It requires a lot of thinking, self-introspection, and meticulous planning. However, unfortunately, this decision is often rushed through, made in an instant, and almost always without the due concern and discussion that it demands.

Current Scenario

As the 10th standard examination (S.S.C / C.B.S.E. / I.C.S.E.) is done, and everyone is awaiting results, a common scenario can be seen in most homes: children and parents having heated, passionate discussions about which stream everyone thinks the child should opt for. Many a time the decision is made purely on the basis marks secured in the S.S.C. examination. Other factors which influence the decision are: current trends, peer impact, what the parents think their child should study (in other words, the parents' wishes), and inputs from relatives, acquaintances, etc.

Up until the 10th standard, a student can very easily secure good marks by means of mere rote learning. But from the 11th standard onwards, things change; rote learning proves to be of almost no use, as the complexity of subjects in the curriculum increases. Additionally, the 12th standard examination, and other competitive entrance exams, which students undertake, contain questions which not only require conceptual knowledge for solving, but also a higher level of applied knowledge. You cannot just rote two plus two equals four; you need to be able to add 365 and 729, for which you need to understand how addition works! It is quite likely that students, who have relied on rote learning in school, will suddenly find it very difficult to cope with their studies, which will in turn affect their performance.

Stream selection after the S.S.C. (Maharashtra State Board) examination requires more consideration. This is because of the "best of five" rule. According to this rule, 5 subjects out of 7, in which the student has secured highest marks, are considered in calculating the overall percentage secured by a student in the S.S.C. examination. This can be misleading when it comes to stream-selection because, a student may meet the cut-off score for a particular stream, in spite of not scoring well in the subjects related to that stream. For example, a student who has secured fewer marks in science and mathematics, can make up for the deficit by scoring better marks in other subjects; his overall marks (according to the 'best of five' rule) may now allow him to secure admission to pursue a Bachelor's degree in Science. However, does such a student truly have the aptitude for science, even though his marks suggest so? No. So what makes students and parents still do something like this? One of the biggest reasons is the general notion that *"Science stream has a lot of scope"*; in other words, *"a bachelor's degree in science improves your chances of building a successful career for yourself"*. This is in fact a myth. Only those who want to do engineering, health sciences, pharmacy and research in pure sciences, need to choose the option for science for the 12ᵗʰ standard examination. There are so many career paths, where having pursued science in 12ᵗʰ standard is not a prerequisite.

Majority of students are not clear about what they want to do, which field they want to work in, build a career in; choosing an appropriate stream becomes a harder task for such students. Sometimes, even if a student is clear about what s/he wants to do, if s/he is not adequately informed, s/he may still end up making the wrong choice. Such students are then 'stuck' with the wrong choice for two years. Ultimately, if they are not able to score well in the 12ᵗʰ standard exam, their chances of securing admission into the chosen course after 12ᵗʰ may be greatly adversely affected. For example, the prerequisite to pursue a Bachelor of Pharmacy (B. Pharm) degree in Maharashtra through the Maharashtra State Common Entrance Test is 12th standard from Science stream with Physics and Chemistry as compulsory subjects along with Mathematics or Biology. Which means that if a student has dropped either mathematics or biology in 11th and 12th standard, s/he is still eligible for admission.

It is of utmost importance for students as well as the parents to weigh all their options properly, before choosing a stream to aid the child to make a career. Several aspects need to be considered to make a proper well-informed decision. First and foremost, students need to seriously and sincerely think about what they like and what they don't. In due course of my interactions with parents, I have realised that parents often disregard their children's opinions. There is a pre-conceived notion in their minds that, a 10th standard student is too young, a mere child of 15-16, to know what s/he likes. But through my experiences, I know that many a time even young children *do* know what they like. More so, they are clearer about what they *do not* like. It is not advisable to simply take a decision on your child's behalf, especially if the child has given things a thought and come up with a plan, or even a single idea or concept. Parents should discuss with their children and find out about their plans, their likes and dislikes, their aspirations… because one wrong choice made at that point, can completely change the track of their life, sometimes with irreversible consequences.

However, it is not quite as simple as that. The word '*like*' can be quite deceiving. When a student says that s/he '*likes*' a particular stream or subject, it's very important to find out whether s/he is truly likes it and would want to pursue a career in it for the rest of her/his working life, or is s/he merely fascinated by the subject/field. I once met a 10th standard student who wanted to become a doctor. When asked why, the very first thing he said was that he liked science; however his marks told a different story! After speaking to him for some time, I understood that – one of his relatives had recently purchased one of his dream cars, and that relative is a doctor. Perhaps, the young boy felt he too will be able to buy the same car at some point if he became a doctor. This is clearly the wrong reason to become a doctor though! Thus, before selecting a stream it's very important to ask yourself why you want to opt for it. One way to monitor the likes and dislikes of a child is to observe the student's marks from the 8th standard onwards. Does the child perform consistently well in a particular subject, and poorly in another? Although not a sole indicator, a child's performance in the different subject taught in school can give parents a good idea about where his/her interests lie, also which subject does the child find easier to grasp.

Second most important factor to consider, is one's own aptitude for a particular stream or subject. A reliable and standardised aptitude test can be very useful to identify a student's abilities, talent or capacity to learn and apply knowledge of a particular subject.

Understanding its usefulness, Maharashtra State Government administered an online aptitude test for 10th standard students schools affiliated to Maharashtra State Board of Secondary and Higher Secondary Education[1] (MSBSHSE) in February 2016. These tests will be conducted in the month of February every year during the practical exams for SSC. The results of these tests will be declared in April or May on the official website of Maharashtra State Board of Secondary and Higher Secondary Education (MSBSHSE).

1.

Aptitude Test

An aptitude test is a type of psychometric assessment that evaluates the talent/ability/potential to perform a certain task. It is an instrument, which is used to determine and measure an individual's ability to acquire, through future training, some specific set of skills. Aptitude tests often include items which measure more specialised abilities--such as cognitive, verbal and numerical etc., that predict scholastic performance in educational programs. The aptitude tests are based on the Structure of Intellect proposed by a renowned psychologist, J. P. Guilford in 1955 and the Theory of Multiple Intelligence proposed by the psychologist, Howard Gardner in 1883.

These tests can be used to help a student in the following ways:

a. Choose among educational and career options based on strengths and weakness
b. Help them understand why they do well or poorly in certain subjects.
c. Can suggest new career options not previously considered
d. Change or raise educational and career aspirations.

However, the aptitude test cannot pinpoint a specific career or a specific subject, they can definitely suggest broad areas in which the individual has abilities to perform well as well as what areas need to be worked on. An aptitude test is a series of questions or statements that one answers or responds to, that are then scored. The results are provided in the form of a report that gives feedback on the interest, abilities, skills, personality etc., depending of the type of test, the student is undergoing.

Applications of Aptitude test in career / stream selection:

A. It portrays a graph of one's psychological and personality traits.

B. It measures various abilities and interests, which reflect a person's strengths and weaknesses. Thus can provide a guideline for selecting an appropriate educational path.

C. For example, a student having excellent 2-dimensional - 3-dimensional ability can make an excellent career in designing or related field. Similarly a student having very good logical reasoning, knowledge and numerical ability, may do very well in computer programming, science or can become a chartered accountant.

The following abilities are usually measured in an aptitude test:

- Cognitive ability - the basic capacity to understand something – understand concepts and build new knowledge on the existing knowledge.

- Reasoning ability - the capacity to apply logic, answer questions like why, how etc. Thus relating to logical thinking and analysing.

- Figural Memory - This ability refers to the capacity of observing minute things, understanding similarities and differences, learning form experiences etc.

- Special ability - This ability refers to the basic understanding of spaces, dimensions, speed, visualising objects in 2D-3D perspective.
- Verbal ability - Refers to the degree of comfort with languages - vocabulary, writing, reading, using correct grammar etc.
- Numerical ability - This ability refers to the ease of using numbers quickly and accurately, applying mathematical formulas.
- Numerical memory - This refers to the ability to concentrate, remember numbers or things around you.

There are different aptitude tests available; some of them are listed below:

- AIM Test by Janaprabodhini, Pune
- Career Futura Aptitude Test
- DBDA (David's Battery of Differential Aptitude)
- DAT (Differential Aptitude Test)

An aptitude test report can provide a basic guideline to a student and his/her parents about their strengths and weaknesses in a particular area. Other factors which also need to be considered while selecting a stream are students' personality and study skills.

A career or educational advisor is a trained professional who assists the student in the process of stream selection and career planning process.

Role of the career/educational advisor:

- Exploring interests, aptitudes, abilities and study skills of the student
- Provide information about different Career options suitable for the student after considering his/her forte.
- Provide information about the different streams and the skills required and entrance examinations required to get admission to a chosen course
- Provide guidance in setting a goal and preparing an action plan.

Let us now take a look at the different streams a child can select after passing the S.S.C. exam; what are the subjects offered in each stream, and which career paths they can lead up to. Before that we will take a general overview of the Indian Educational System.

> Everybody is a genius. But if you judge a fish by its ability to climb a tree, it will live its whole life believing that it is STUPID!!
>
> - Albert Einstein

2

Overview of the current educational system in India

The Central Board and most state boards in India follow the "10+2+3" pattern of education. The Secondary School Certificate is awarded after completing 10th standard, while Higher Secondary Certificate is awarded after 12th standard. After this, a student can pursue graduation for three years in a selected stream, typically Science, Commerce or Arts / Humanities, at the end of which the student is awarded a Bachelor's degree. Some professional courses have longer durations; thereby enabling the student with "10+2+4" years (as in case of Bachelor of Engineering, or B.E. degree), or "10+2+5" years (as in case of Bachelor of Architecture, or B.Arch. degree) of formal education.

The Master's degree is typically awarded after additional 2 years of formal education. Again, as with the Bachelor's degree, certain Master's degrees are awarded after 3 or more years; for example, some health science courses like Doctor of Medicine (MD), Master of Surgery (MS), Master of Physiotherapy (M.P.T.H.), Master of Dental Surgery (M.D.S.) etc.

For students who do not wish to follow this path, certain certificate and diploma courses offer an alternative path. The prerequisite for most of these courses is either an S.S.C. or an H.S.C. certificate. The main focus of these courses is on skill development and opening the avenues for employability. Some diploma courses also offer a lateral entry to conventional degree programs. The Engineering Diploma, is an example of such a course. Another example is that of the Minimum Competency Vocational Course (M.C.V.C.), a two-year certificate course that one can opt for after 10th standard. The focus of this course is on developing vocational skills. Typically, these courses cost much less than their conventional bachelor's degree counterparts. Another option is that of obtaining certification from Industrial Training Institute. Duration of these courses ranges from one to three years, depending on the subject area.

Thus, a student, completing his/her school education up to 10ᵗʰ standard (Secondary School Certificate), can opt for the following streams:

- Science
- Commerce
- Arts/Humanities
- Home Science
- Diploma
- Vocational Certificate Courses, such as ITI (Industrial Training Institute) or MCVC (Minimum Competency Vocational Courses)

Graduation after 10+2 can be further classified into professional and non-professional courses. The following flowchart explains the educational paths available as per the Indian educational system:

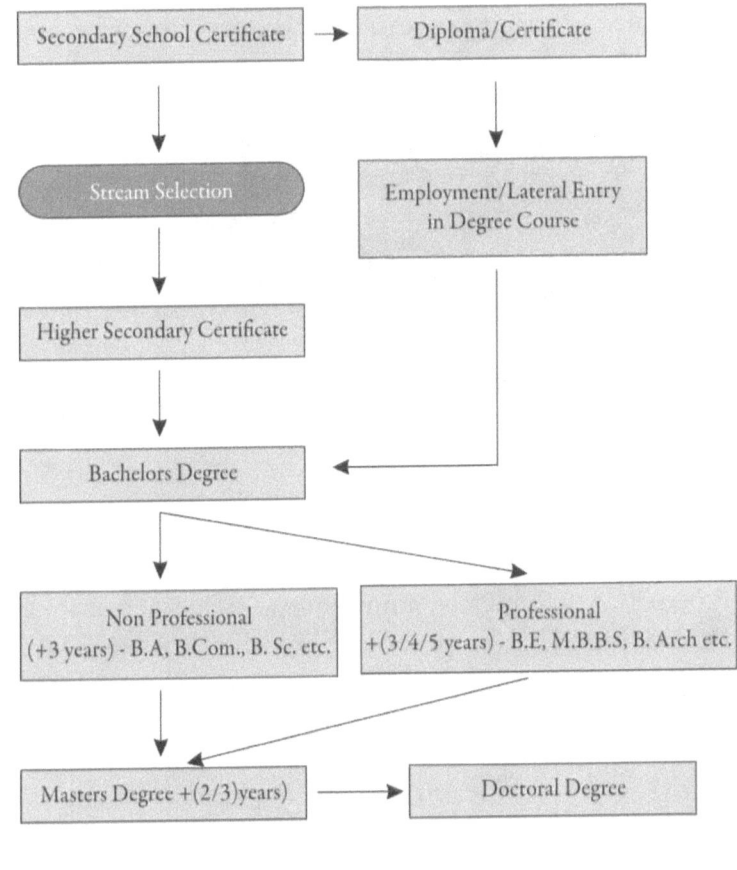

Chart: 2.1

Overview of different streams available in 11ᵗʰ and 12ᵗʰ standard:

Currently, our education system allows students to select only one stream from the available set of streams. A student can then choose subjects available in that particular stream; s/he can't choose subjects from other streams. The next few years are of their educational journey towards career development.

> If you are walking down the right path and you are willing to keep walking, eventually you will make progress!!
>
> -Barack Obama

The flowchart below gives an overview of the different streams, and subjects under each stream, available in the 11th standard in Maharashtra State.

Admissions to the Arts, Science, and Commerce stream for the 11th standard are given through the Common Application Process (CAP). Similarly, admissions to technical courses like Diploma and ITI also processed through a separate CAP for these streams. Students seeking admission to the MCVC courses need to apply to the respective college/s individually.

Streams after 10th Standard

Science	Commerce	Psychology Sociology Philosophy	Home Science	Diploma	MCVC	ITI	IB Diploma
Physics Chemistry English 2nd language/ IT Options: Math/Bio/ Geography/ (Math + Vocational)	English Accounts Economics O. C. Second language/IT Options: Math/S. P.	English 2nd language/IT Options: Any 4 from History Geography Political Sci. Economics Psychology Sociology Philosophy Logic Math	English, Marathi/ Hindi. Psychology. Chem./Bio.. Physical Education. Home Management	Engineering: Civil. IT, E and TC. Electrical. Electronics. Computers and others Fine Arts: GD Arts	Engineering and Technology. Business and Commerce. Catering and Food Tech.. Paramedical. Agriculture. Fisheries		

Chart: 2.2

15

2.1

Science Stream

The 11th standard (First Year Junior College, F.Y.J.C.) admissions cut-offs in some of the popular colleges in Pune indicate that the science stream is still the most opted-for stream. In Chart no. 2.2, we have seen that there are only three compulsory subjects in the Science stream for 11th and 12th standard, viz. English, Physics, and Chemistry. We have also seen the career paths arising from the selected set of subjects. We will discuss them in detail in the later part of this book. First, let us take a look at the optional subjects available, and how to decide which subjects one should opt out of.

The first and the most important optional subject to consider is *Mathematics*. Many students, especially those interested in going into the Health Sciences stream after 12th standard ask me, *Can I drop Mathematics?* The answer is, "*as far as possible NO*". The reason for this is - Mathematics compliments Physics, which is a compulsory subject. Furthermore, it can also help in biostatistics in future. However, those who want to pursue Engineering can think of dropping Biology; this frees up a lot of time considering they have one less subject to study, and considering that Biology has theory as well as laboratory practical classes.

The next optional subject is the second language. Those students who plan to appear for the various entrance examinations already have a lot of burden of preparations. Hence it would be a good idea to choose a language which they have studied previously. Learning a new language will unnecessarily burden them with one more subject.

Bifocal subjects: Those who wish to enter the Engineering branch for graduation may prefer to opt for a Bifocal subject. A bifocal subject carries 200 marks; thus opting for a bifocal subject allows a student to drop the second language and biology. The student thus has one subject less to worry about. The bifocal subjects that are offered in the science stream are:

i.	Electronics
ii.	Computer Science
iii.	Scooter Motorcycle Servicing (SMS)

iv.	Electrical Maintenance
v.	Mechanical Maintenance
vi.	Civil Engineering

Another advantage of the Bifocal subjects is that the student directly gets admission to the Second Year Engineering Diploma course in the area which is closely related to the Bifocal subject s/he opts for. For example, a student who has chosen Computer Science as a Bifocal subject will be eligible for admission to the Computer Science Diploma program if all other prerequisites are fulfilled. The major disadvantage of opting for a Bifocal subject, however, is that you close almost all other career options in health science, biotechnology or biology-related fields. This may be a cause of concern for students who are still not sure about which field they want to choose for their graduation.

Careers arising ONLY from the Science Stream:

The different science-related career paths that originate post 12th standard, each of which has a different set of prerequisites. Some require the student to have studied 12th standard Physics, Chemistry, and Mathematics; some other courses require 12th standard Physics, Chemistry, and Biology. There are some career pathways which have certain prerequisites for e.g. to get into Engineering, Physics, Chemistry and Mathematics (PCM) are compulsory subjects in 11th and 12th, on the other hand, Mathematics is not compulsory for Health Sciences but Physics, Chemistry and Biology (PCB) are, while for Pharmacy, Physics and Chemistry are compulsory but one should have either Mathematics or Biology. Chart 2.1.1 gives an overview of the career paths based on their prerequisites: (A) PCM Careers (Physics, Chemistry, and Mathematics), (B) PCB Careers (Physics, Chemistry, and Biology), and (C) PCMB Careers (Physics, Chemistry, Mathematics, and Biology).

Chart 2.1.1

Career Paths ONLY from Science Stream

PCM	PCB	PCM+B/ PCM/B*
Engineering	Medical (MBBS)	Indian Army
Indian Air Force	Dental	Pharmacy
Indian Navy	Ayurved	Biotechnology
Merchant Navy	Homeopathy	Environmental Science
Commercial Pilot	Unani	Computer Science
	Physiotherapy	Computer Animation
	Occupation Therapy	
	Paramedical	
	Agriculture	
	Microbiology	
	Veterinary	

*Either PCM & B or PC + M or B

(A) PCM Careers:

The major careers belonging to this group are Engineering, Indian Air Force, Indian Navy, Merchant Navy, Commercial Pilot, etc. This means that, a student will become eligible for admission or to appear for the entrance examination (whichever is applicable) for these courses, ONLY if s/he has studied Physics, Chemistry, and Mathematics in 11ᵗʰ and 12ᵗʰ standard. Other subjects would be English, which is compulsory in the science stream. The optional subjects may be either a second language, or either one of Information Technology, Biology, and Geography. Finally, if a student does not wish to elect a second language and an optional subject, s/he may choose either one of the 200-marks Bifocal.

(B) PCB Careers:

The major careers belonging to the PCB group are Medicine, Dentistry, Ayurveda, Nursing, Physiotherapy, Agriculture, Microbiology, etc. This means that, a student will become eligible for admission, or to appear for the entrance examination (whichever is applicable), ONLY if s/he has studied Physics, Chemistry, and Biology in 11ᵗʰ and 12ᵗʰ standard. Other subjects would be English, which is compulsory in the science stream. The second optional subject could be a second language or Information Technology; the third optional subject could be Mathematics or Geography. A student cannot opt for any of the bifocal subjects.

The biggest dilemma for students following the PCB group is whether or not to choose Mathematics. Most of the students who choose PCB wish to drop Mathematics. However, it is not advisable to do so, for two reasons. First, as already mentioned, dropping Mathematics makes studying Physics a harder task to manage. The second reason is: admissions to graduate courses are done at college level, and so prerequisites may slightly vary. For some subjects like Computer Science or Biotechnology, a college may have 12ᵗʰ standard Mathematics as a prerequisite. Thus, dropping Mathematics can limit your choice of college. Also, some of the B.Sc. Agriculture courses require their students to make up for not having studied Mathematics in 12ᵗʰ standard, by electing it as a subject in the first year of their course. (More information on Agriculture course is given in the separate chapter on Agriculture).

(C) PCMB Careers:

As stated earlier, there is no central admission procedure for graduate courses; admissions are done to the discretion of respective college. University of Pune does NOT have Mathematics as a prerequisite for admission/appearance for entrance exam for the B.Sc. Biotechnology course. However, a college may choose to have Mathematics as its prerequisite. This is why some students opt to go with the PCMB stream, whereby they study Physics, Chemistry, Mathematics, and Biology; along with English (compulsory subject) and a second language or Information Technology. Students studying Biotechnology also have to study subjects like Mathematics and Statistical Methods, Physics, Computers and Applications, Bioinformatics, along with Biology- and Chemistry-related subjects. Having a mathematics background makes study of these subjects much simpler. Apart from Biotechnology, students interested in studying Microbiology may also choose to elect Mathematics for 11th-12th standard. During the course of the graduate Microbiology program, students study Biostatistics for a semester. It is often easier to manage that subject if you have a background of Mathematics; in fact, with a little bit of effort, one can score well in the subject as it is not a descriptive subject. Thus, opting for PCMB group can prove to be a very sound and wise decision.

2.2

Commerce Stream

Commerce is the world of money, trade, business, accounting, audit, costing, economics, and various trends that govern these aspects of human life. It also covers the upcoming fields like E-Commerce, Financial Markets, Fiscal Policies, Market Analysis, and other. The overall economic growth analysis of a country depends on advance commerce research and analysis. Thus this stream offers a wide range of career options. Students who are interested to pursue such careers may opt for the Commerce Stream. The Commerce stream opens pathways to various career avenues. The beauty of commerce stream is, that it is a multidisciplinary field that offers a wide array of career options after 12th standard. But still it is recommended that a student should first find out what s/he would like to study, whether s/he has the aptitude to understand the subjects offered in the commerce stream and then select the options accordingly.

Commerce opens up many career avenues in auditing, accounting, costing, banking, trading etc. The major sought after careers in Commerce are: Chartered Accountant (CA), Company Secretary (CS), Cost and Works Professional (CWA, formerly ICWA), Chartered Financial Analyst (CFA), or a Management degree in Finance after completing graduation.

The advantage of choosing commerce stream is that one gets enough time as the duration of college classes is comparatively less than that of science stream, there are no practical classes. Hence this time can be utilised in skill and knowledge building to increase employability in future. Those who are interested in pursuing the professional careers like chartered accountancy, company secretary or cost accountancy etc. utilise the time in preparing for these. If not these, many other less intense and less rigorous complementary courses can also be pursued, even after completing regular college hours, and allotting time for self-study, viz. diploma in Insurance sales and marketing, certification as Accounting Technician, certification in Tally, certification in Cyber security, or other courses offered by National Institute of Securities Markets, Association of Mutual Funds, or other comparative institute. Another option would be to pursue a foreign language. Trade and commerce is no longer local in our country, and knowing a foreign language always proves to be an asset. One can choose a course depending on his/her aptitude in a particular area, and the final qualification that one is seeking.

Handy tips:

- The commerce syllabus and course are not as intense as that of science; this leaves a student with a lot of free time, as compared to a science student. It is easy to while away this time and lose focus. However, it is advisable to use this extra time productively, in gaining skills that will aid overall development and make you an all-rounder. It is also necessary to perform well in the course, and keep up the average marks obtained in 10th standard, throughout 11th -12th and even during graduation. Ideally, one should aim at increasing the average marks obtained by at least 1-2 per cent every year.

- Many commerce subjects are descriptive hence it is also advised to practice reading and writing extensively.

Overview of some of the subjects in the commerce stream:

Organisation of Commerce and Management (O.C.): This subject explains the techniques to choose appropriate form of business and gives information about the various services required to support a business – transportation, storage & warehousing, marketing, financing etc. It familiarises students with the growing importance of social responsibilities of a business, and also with the rights of a consumer under the Consumer Protection Act. Additionally, it guides students on management principles, thus laying a foundation of management skills.

Secretarial Practice (S.P.): Secretarial Practice is a subject that compiles the knowledge and skills a Company Secretary should posses. The competency of the company secretary lies in conducting valid correspondence between the Board of Directors and the public, thereby acts as a front face of the organization.

Accountancy: Accountancy is an integral part of commerce stream. It is a branch of Mathematics concerned with the financial aspect of a business. In accountancy, students learn the techniques of recording, classifying, and summarising financial transactions and events, and interpreting the results of these transactions; typically, and most importantly, whether a transaction lead to profit, or loss, or neither.

Economics: In economics, one gains knowledge about the impact of trade between different organisations, countries, and industries. It basically deals with understanding how the world economy or government policies impact the public, industries, and nations, and employment of the people that make up a company, or country.

Career Paths after 12th Commerce

Chartered Accountant Company Secretary Cost Accountant Chartered Financial Analyst Bachelor in Business Administration (BBA) Bachelor in Business Administration - International Business (BBM-IB) B.Com. + Additional Skill Development alongside	NDA (Army) Architecture and Design (Fashion, Graphic, Product etc) Fine Arts Law Hotel Management Computer Applications (BCA)

Chart: 2.2.1

2.3

Arts / Humanities Stream:

Humanities Stream encompasses topics like literature, social sciences, philosophy, etc. – as you may have observed, these subjects are concerned with human ideas and behaviour; hence the name 'Humanities'. The main focus of Humanities is human beings, and the society. The different subject, explore different aspects of human life, viz. social, cultural, political, economic etc. Humanities take on a mainly analytical, critical, or exploratory look at the world. Humanities offer a wide range of career options after 12th standard. The important subjects included in the Arts/Humanities stream are Languages / Literature, Economics, History, Geography, Psychology, Sociology, and Political Science. Usually students choose this stream when they have a specific interest. For e.g. psychology, languages, journalism, law, mass communication, hotel management, political science etc. As per my experience, I have seen that the students, choosing the Humanities stream have taken an informed decision.

So far we have seen that some career paths have a specific subject prerequisite; a deficit in the prerequisite can lead to non-eligibility for admission. Hence it is important to find out about the subject requirement well in advance, before selecting a stream and plan accordingly. For example, the entry requirement for Indian Army is 12th pass with English and Mathematics from any stream, hence if you are planning to appear for the NDA entrance only for Army, and you plan to opt for the commerce stream in 11th and 12th, then it is very important to choose Mathematics as one of the subjects in the 11ᵗʰ and 12ᵗʰ.

The charts below give an overview of different career paths and their required streams.

Career paths after 12ᵗʰ in Arts & Humanities

Languages and Literature

Psychology

Sociology

Political Science

Economics

Mathematics

History

Geography

Anthropology

Library and Information Science

Archeology and Museology

NDA (Army)

Architecture and Design
(Fashion, Graphic, Product etc)

Fine Arts

Law

Hotel Management

Computer Applications (BCA)

Journalism

Mass Communication

Chart: 2.3.1

Careers that require Science Stream in 12th standard

Indian Air Force and Navy	Research in Pure Sciences	Health Sciences
Engineering and Technology	Biotechnology	Paramedical
Commercial Pilot	Bioinformatics	Pharmacy
Merchant Navy	Computer Science	Veterinary
Atomic Energy	Animation	Agriculture Science
Nanotechnology	Electronics	Environmental Science
Astronomy	Renewable	Geology
		Microbiology
		Neuroscience

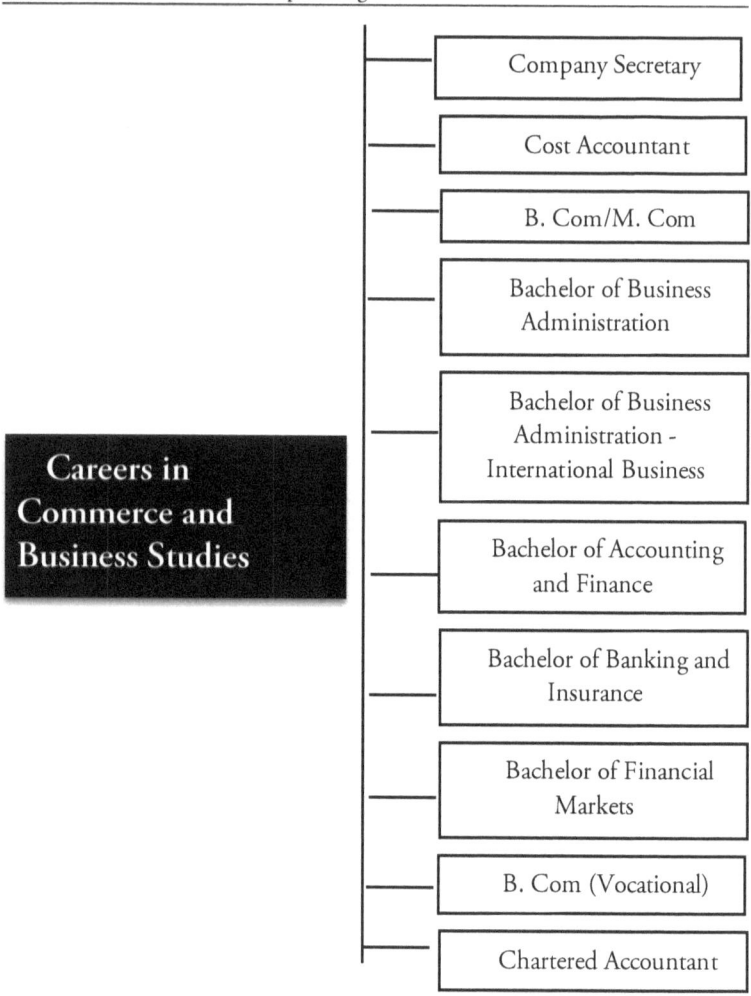

Note:

For diploma or graduate degree in commerce, the required eligibility criteria is "10/10+2" from ANY stream. To apply for Masters of Commerce (M.Com.), the prerequisite is a graduate degree in commerce (B.Com.). Hence, up until graduation, there is no subject prerequisite for commerce – any student who has successfully cleared the 12th standard is eligible. But of course, it is only logical to build a foundation in 12th standard itself, if one is sure about opting for commerce for graduation. This makes preparation for the selected career path easy.

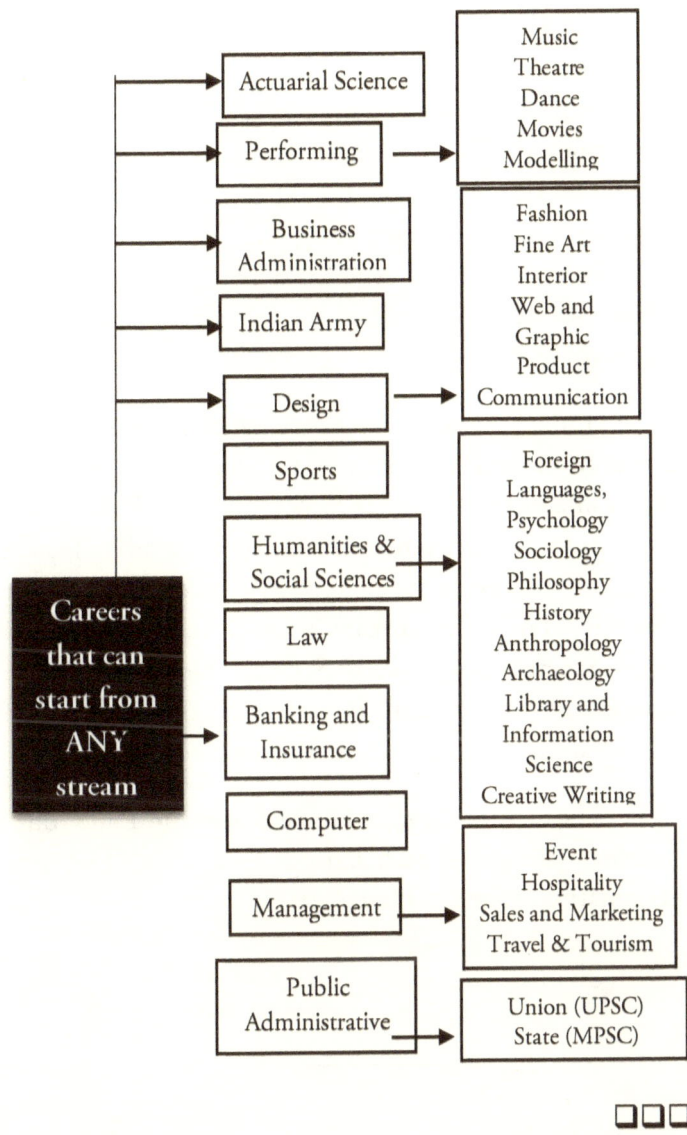

2.4

Home Science

The Home Science stream is available only for girls after 10th standard. There are four mandatory and two elective subjects in this stream in the 11th and 12th standard. The mandatory subjects are English, Psychology, Physical Education, and Home Management. The elective subjects include one language (either Marathi or Hindi), and either Chemistry or Biology.

The Home Science stream offers a wide array of career paths ranging from the Undergraduate till Doctorate level. There are nine Home Science colleges in Mumbai and Pune which are affiliated to the Shreemati Nathibai Damodar Thackersey (S.N.D.T.) University, Mumbai[2], India's first Women's University. The various stream in which courses are offered are Home Science, Arts, Social Science, Fine Art, Education, Library and Information Science, Commerce, Technology, Law, Management, Science, Pharmacy, and Nursing.

The S.N.D.T. College of Home Science in Pune[3] offers six bachelor's programs, each lasting three years. The different specialisations that are offered are:

---

[2] http://sndt.ac.in
[3] http://sndthsc.com/

31

i. Bachelors in Human Ecology and Consumer Services:

This is a composite course offering subjects in a variety of disciplines like, cookery, garment construction, household equipment, orientation to early childhood education, consumer and market, leadership, dyeing and printing, food preservation, child nutrition, and entrepreneurship development.

This course aims at enabling students to become "Entrepreneurs". Every year, study tours are conducted to various organisations, where self-employment and community development are the main predominant theme. Workshops and seminars on Entrepreneurial capacity Building are also organised.

Eligibility: 10+2 years of education from any stream, with English

ii. Bachelors in Nutrition and Dietetics:

Students are trained in the fields of nutrition and dietetics, community nutrition, and patient counselling. Upon graduation, students can work as dieticians in hospitals, health clubs, etc.

Eligibility: 10+2 years of education from any stream, with English

iii. Bachelor of Science in Food Science and Quality Control:

The course aims at training students in food processing, new product development, sensory evaluation, and quality control. Some of the subjects taught are: Physiology and Reproductive health, Physical and Analytical Chemistry, Human Ecology and Family Science, Food Microbiology and Preservation, Nutrition, Diet Therapy, Culinary Services, etc. Students can work in food industries, food analytical laboratories, or become entrepreneurs.

Eligibility: 10+2 years of education from any stream, with English

iv. Bachelor of Science in Family Resource Management (Interior Space Design):

This course focuses on enabling students to gain a good understanding of the principles of interior design and skill required in planning interior spaces, as well as executing and managing projects. The first three semesters comprise of a unique blend of subjects taken from different areas of Home Science curriculum. Resource Management and Art, Design and Aesthetics are the foundation courses offered.

Eligibility: 10+2 years of education from any stream, with English. However, admission to the desired specialisation is given in the second year, on the basis of merit.

v. Bachelor in Human Development:

This is also a very comprehensive course. Students can select this specialisation in the second year of the general course, which is merit based. This course covers different subjects like Lifespan Development, Guidance and Counselling, Children with Special Needs, Child Psychology, etc. A Master's degree in any of these subjects opens up a lot of avenues for students, typically in the field of human development, school counselling, clinical psychology, counselling psychology, etc.

Eligibility: 10+2 years of education from any stream, with English. Admission to the desired specialisation is given in the second year, on the basis of merit.

vi. **Bachelor of Science in Textile Science and Apparel Design:**

The subjects included in this graduate program include Textile Science, Wet Processing, Textile Chemistry, Fabric Manufacture, Textile and Garment Quality Control, Fashion Illustration, Grading, Traditional Textiles and Embroideries of India, Fashion Apparel Design, Apparel Merchandising, and Application of IT in Textile Science and Apparel Design.

Eligibility: 10+2 years of education from any stream, with English. Admission to the desired specialisation depends on performance in entrance test for the same, conducted at the end of the first year.

In addition to these courses there are different courses offered by the university in different streams. The list below gives an overview of these:

Table 2.4.1

#	Stream	Degree
1	Home Science	B.Sc. (Food Science and Nutrition/Resource Management/Human Development/Textiles Science/Extension Education)
2	Arts	B.A.(English/Hindi/Gujrati/Marathi/Sanskrit), Bachelor of Mass Media
3	Social Science	B.A.(Geography/History/Political Science/Economics /Sociology/Psychology), Bachelor of Social Work (B.S.W.)
4	Fine Art	B.A.(Music), Bachelor of Visual Art (B.V.A.)
5	Education	B.Ed.(Education), B.Ed.(Special Education)
6	Library and Information Science	Bachelor of Library and Information Science (B.L.I.Sc.)
7	Commerce	B. Com.
8	Technology	B.C.A.(Computer Applications), Computer Science, Electronics, Electronics and Telecommunications, Information Technology
9	Law	Bachelor of Law (LLB), Bachelor of Business Administration (BBA)
10	Management	Bachelor of Management Studies (B.M.S.)
11	Science	B.Sc. (Physics / Chemistry / Botany / Zoology / Information Technology
12	Pharmacy	Bachelor of Pharmacy (B. Pharm)
13	Nursing	B.Sc. Nursing

2.5

Diploma Courses after 10th or 12th Standard

A wide array of diploma programs is currently available after 10th or 12th standard, in our education system. A diploma program focuses more on practical skill building rather than theoretical knowledge. The focus of the curriculum is on how to handle the technicalities of a job, the curriculum is aligned with on-the-job situations. Some of the diploma curricula have a short internship as a part of the program.

There are two broad types of diploma programs - Engineering and non-Engineering. The Engineering diplomas are approved by the All India Council for Technical Education, Govt. of India (AICTE)[4]. Most of the Engineering diplomas are of 3-year duration. There are some 4-year Industry-Integrated Diplomas, which have integrated industrial training as a part of the curriculum, commonly known as Sandwich Pattern. The non-engineering diploma programs are of 2-year duration. Currently, there are about 50 different diplomas in engineering faculty and 25 diplomas in other faculties offered by the Maharashtra State Board of Technical Education (MSBTE)[5]. In addition to these, there are some Post-Graduate diplomas, which one is eligible for only after first obtaining a Bachelor's degree. Table No. 2.5.1 below gives the list of the

---

[4] http://www.aicte-india.org
[5] http://www.msbte.com/

broad subject groups in which the AICTE approved diplomas are offered.

Engineering Diploma (after 10th standard): (Table No. 2.5.1)

#	Subject Group	Branches
1	Civil Engineering	Civil-Rural, Construction Technology, Civil-Environment
2	Chemical Engineering	Chemical, Plastic
3	Computer Engineering	Computer Technology, Information Technology, Computer Science
4	Electronics Engineering	Digital Electronics, Electronics and Communication, Telecommunication
5	Electrical Engineering	Electrical, Electrical and Power, Electrical and Electronics
6	Instrumentation Engineering	Instrumentation and Control
7	Mechanical Engineering	Automobile, Fabrication Technology, Production, Mechanical, Plant Tech.
8	Metallurgy Engineering	Metallurgy
9	Mining Engineering	Mining Engineering, Mining and Mine Surveying
10	Printing Engineering	Printing Technology

#	Subject Group	Branches
11	Special Engineering	Dress Designing and Garment Manufacturing, Food Technology, Leather Goods and Footwear Technology, Leather Technology, Medical Laboratory Technology, Travel and Tourism, Plastic Polymer Engineering, Sugar Manufacturing
12	Textile Engineering	Fashion and Clothing Technology, Garment Technology, Knitting Technology, Man-made Fiber Manufacture, Man-made Textile Technology, Textile Technology
13	Agriculture Engineering	
14	Foreign Collaboration	Automotive Technology
15	Architecture Assistantship	

The Engineering diploma programs are generally of 3-year duration. Upon completion, they allow for a student to gain lateral entry to the second year of engineering degree course. So, there are two options available for a student who wants to pursue engineering: either s/he can complete 12th standard from the required stream, then give the required entrance exam, and get admission to the desired college for obtaining a bachelor's degree (the 10+2+4 pattern); or s/he may opt to get a diploma directly after 10th standard, and then gain lateral entry into the bachelor's program, and then complete the program and obtain the bachelor's degree (the 10+3+3 pattern). Either way, it takes six years after completing 10th standard, to get a bachelor's degree in engineering.

Admission process for diploma programs:

Admissions to all government, as well as most private diploma courses are given through Centralised Admission Process (CAP). A notification about the details of the admission process is posted on the Directorate of Technical Education (DTE)[6] website. A student has to submit only one application form, and the seats are allotted on the basis of merit. District-wise preference is given to students – a student belonging to a particular district has first preference to 70% seats in his/her district. Remaining 30% seats are secured for students from other districts in Maharashtra. 20% seats are reserved for management quota in the private colleges. Information about the approved colleges, courses and number of seats available in each college and the admission procedure is available on the DTE website.

Many a time students are confused about whether to choose a diploma course after 10th standard, or to opt for an engineering degree after 12th standard. Let's see the advantages and disadvantages of choosing a diploma course after 10th standard.

---

[6] http://www.dtemaharashtra.gov.in

Advantages	Disadvantages
When you choose the diploma course after 10ᵗʰ, you skip the phase of tension and uncertainty of the entrance test and engineering admissions.	One has to choose the diploma branch (Mechanical/Electrical/Computer etc) in the first year itself and has to continue with it even in the degree program if opted for.
One can directly get a job or become an entrepreneur after diploma.	As the diploma students skip 11ᵗʰ and 12ᵗʰ standard, they can't explore other subjects like Biology, Biotechnology, etc.
Lateral entry to engineering degree is possible. Similarly, one can also pursue, A.M.I.E., B.Tech., D.B.M., B.B.A., B.C.A.	There is a tough competition to get into the degree course after completing diploma. One has to really work hard to get good marks.
The lateral entry to engineering degree program is without any CET	The student has no control on which degree college to choose for the lateral entry.

Non-Engineering Diploma Programs, approved by Maharashtra Government (after 10ᵗʰ standard):

There are about 25 non-engineering diploma programs. The duration of these courses is one to two years. These programs are also classified in different groups.

Table No.2.5.2

#	Subject Group	Examples
1	Architecture, Building Construction, Interior Design	Interior Design and Decoration,
2	Computer and Information Technology	3D Animation and Graphics,
3	Beauty Culture	Beauty Culture and Hair Dressing,
4	Fashion Technology	Dress Designing and Manufacturing, Textile Design
5	Learn and Earn Scheme	Industrial Drug Science, Food Science, Retail Management

AICTE Approved Diploma Programs after 12th standard:

The list below shows AICTE approved Diploma Programs after 12th standard. The admission process is centralised, through the Directorate of Technical Education.

Table No.2.5.3

#	Diploma Program	Eligibility
1	Hotel Management and Catering Technology	10+2(English+ Science/Arts/Commerce/Home Science/ MCVC)
2	Surface Coating Technology	10+2(English + Physics + Chemistry + Mathematics)
3	Rubber Technology	10+2(English + Physics + Chemistry + Mathematics) Or Engineering Diploma
4	Pharmacy	10+2(English + Physics + Chemistry + Mathematics/Biology)

Maharashtra Government Approved Diploma Programs after 12ᵗʰ standard:

Table No.2.5.4

#	Diploma Program	Eligibility
1	Computer Hardware and Networking	10+2(English+ Science/Arts/Commerce/Home Science/ MCVC)
2	Fire Service Engineering	10+2(English+ Science/Arts/Commerce/Home Science/ MCVC)
3	Operation Theatre Technician	10+2(English + Physics + Chemistry + Biology)
4	Hemodialysis Technician	10+2(English + Physics + Chemistry + Biology)
5	Maritime Catering	10+2(English+ Science/Arts/Commerce/Home Science/ MCVC)
6	Hotel Operation	10+2(English+ Science/Arts/Commerce/Home Science/ MCVC)
7	Digital Photography and Digital Graphics	10+2(English+ Science/Arts/Commerce/Home Science/ MCVC)
8	Fruit Processing and Wine Technology	10+2(English+ Science/Arts/Commerce/Home Science/ MCVC)
9	Insurance (Life/Health/Bank/ General)	10+2(English+ Science/Arts/Commerce/Home Science/ MCVC)
10	Aircrafts Maintenance	10+2(English + Physics + Chemistry + Mathematics)

2.6

Minimum Competency Vocational Certificate (MCVC) Stream:

The MCVC stream is commonly known as Vocational Stream. The vocational subjects were introduced by the Directorate of Vocational Education and Training (DVET)[7] with an idea to increase employability, especially employability or self-employability, among the youth. The Vocational Stream focuses on skill building after the 10th standard. The main objectives of the Vocational course are:

- To equip the youth for suitable industrial, self- and wage-employment through well designed formal and non-formal Vocational Education and Training programmes at various institutes.
- To ensure a steady flow of skilled workers in different trades for the industry.
- To raise the quality and quantity of industrial production by systematic training of workers.
- To reduce unemployment among the educated youth by equipping them for suitable industrial employment.

Individual colleges have their own admission process for MCVC courses; there is no centralised procedure/entrance exam. Thus a student interested in joining the MCVC course

---

[7] http://www.dvet.gov.in

in a particular college should contact the admissions department of the respective college.

Course Structure:

- 70% of the course curriculum focuses on skills building and 30% on knowledge building in a particular subject.
- The MCVC curriculum has 6 broad subject groups, which have different courses under them. A student can select one subject from the subject groups. For e.g. a student can select 'Automobile Technology' subject from the 'Technical' subject group. (See Table No.2.6.1). Overall, there are 20 courses under these groups.
- The compulsory subjects for ALL courses are - two languages and one General Foundation subject. Rest of the subjects are related to the course the student has selected
- The student appears for the final examination (12th standard), conducted by the HSC Board where the student has studied.
- Students passing the 12th standard exam can work as Vocational Technician for one year where s/he receives some remuneration as well. The Board of Apprenticeship Training[8] provides assistance to such students (**http://www.apprentice-engineer.com**)
- After passing the 12th standard MCVC examination, students can also pursue an undergraduate degree in BA, B.Com, BBM, B.Sc. (Computer Science), B.Sc.

---

[8] http://www.apprentice-engineer.com

Home Science, B.Sc. Paramedical etc. or to the recently introduced Bachelor of Vocational (B. Voc.) degree.

- Additionally, those who have passed 12th standard from the Technical Group, a direct, lateral entry to the second year of Technical Diploma program is possible. 2% seats are reserved for such students in the diploma colleges.

H.S.C Vocational subjects:

Table No. 2.6.1

#	Group	Subjects
1	Technical	Electronics Technology, Mechanical Technology, Automobile Technology, Construction Technology, Computer Technology
	Commerce	Logistics and Supply Chain Management, Marketing Retail Management, Accounting and Financial Office Management, Banking-Financial Services-Insurance
	Agriculture	Horticulture, Crop Science, Animal Husbandry and Dairy Technology
	Fisheries	Fishery Technology
	Paramedical	Ophthalmic Technician, Radiology Technician, Medical Laboratory Technician, Child-Old Age and Healthcare Service
	Home Science	Food Production, Tourism and Hospitality Management

Note: There are around 1500 aided or unaided colleges offering MCVC courses all over Maharashtra, with a cumulative 80,000 seats.

2.7

Industrial Training Institutes (ITI)

The oldest institutes providing technical training and skill-building opportunities are the Industrial Training Institutes (ITIs) – government-run training organisations. The objective of ITI courses is to provide technical manpower to industries. The students are trained in basic skills required to do jobs like operator, craftsman, etc. Duration of the course varies from one year to three years, depending on the trade opted.

Applications are accepted for 10 days after the 10th standard results are out. The admissions are merit based.

Table No. 2.7.1

#	Subject	Yrs	#	Subject	Yrs
1	Tool and Dye	3	12	Foundry Men	1
2	Machine Tools	3	13	Mason	1
3	Wireman	2	14	Welder	1
4	Painter	2	15	Plumber	1
5	Refrigeration and	2	16	Cutting and Sewing	1
6	Electronics	2	17	Photographer	1
7	Turner	2	18	Stenography (English)	1
8	Electroplater	2	19	Secretarial Practice	1
9	Civil Mechanic	2	20	Desktop Publishing	1
10	Diesel Mechanic	1	21	Computer Operator	1
11	Carpenter	1	22	Stenography	1

After successful completion of training, the person is eligible to appear in the All India Trade Test (AITT) conducted by National Council for Vocational Training (NCVT). After passing AITT, the person is awarded National Trade Certificate (NTC) in concerning trade by NCVT. After passing out from ITI, a person may opt to undergo practical training in his trade in an industry for a year or two. Again the person has to appear and pass in a test to be conducted by NCVT to get the National Apprenticeship Certificate. There are both government-funded, and self-financing ITI's in India.

More than 400 ITI institutes exist in Maharashtra alone, offering more than 75000 seats under 89 different trades. Some ITIs are adopted by industries, and are thus well-equipped in terms of technology and resource persons (trainers). For students, who are looking for vocational training to increase their employability, Vocational Certificates or Diploma program is a good choice.

2.8

International Baccalaureate (IBDP) after 10th standard

The **International Baccalaureate Diploma Programme** (IBDP) is a 2-year educational programme primarily aimed at students aged 16–19. The program provides an internationally accepted qualification to its students, making them eligible for entry into many universities world-wide for higher education.

Initially, International Baccalaureate (IB) as a curriculum started gaining recognition among many parents intending to send their children abroad for higher studies, the main reason being that IB is an internationally recognised diploma program. But now a day it is gradually emerging as one more alternative to the other equivalent boards in India. This is mainly because of the many advantages the IB Diploma curriculum provides. In addition, the Association of Indian Universities (AIU)[9] has conferred equivalence to IBDP, thus making IB Diploma holders eligible for the courses offered by several Indian Universities and Institutes, viz. IIT, IISER, AICTE, COA, etc. and the required entrance exams. Currently there are now about 107 schools offering IBDP in India. Out of these, Pune has 7 schools and there are about 10 schools in Mumbai. The schools in Pune are:

---

[9] http://www.aiu.ac.in

Table No. 2.8.1

#	Name	URL
1	D.Y. Patil International College, Lohegaon	http://www.internationalcollege.in
2	Indus International School, Bhukum	http://www.indusschoolpune.com
3	International School Aamby, Lonavala	http://www.internationalschoolaamby.com
4	UWC Mahindra College, Mulshi	http://uwcmahindracollege.org
5	Mercedes-Benz International School, Hinjewadi	http://mbis.org
6	Symbiosis International School, Viman Nagar	http://symbiosisinternationalschool.net
7	Victorious Kidss Educares, Kharadi	http://www.victoriouskidsseducares.org

The IBDP:

- The IBDP is practical and application-based.
- It has broader spectrum of subjects that lead to all-round development
- The purpose of IBDP is to produce global citizens. But it is quite well integrated with the Indian curriculum as well; Hindi is offered as a second language in IBDP.
- Subjects: There are six subject groups from which a student has to select 6 subjects plus 3 core IB courses are compulsory which the students study for 2 years of the Diploma. These are - Theory of Knowledge, Extended Essay (4000-word independent research

50

paper) and CAS (Creativity, Action and Service). The six subject groups are:

- o Group 1: First Language (English and other international languages, e.g. - Mandarin)
- o Group 2: Second Language (Hindi, French, German, Spanish, Urdu etc.)
- o Group 3: Individuals and Societies (History, Economics, Psychology, Business and Management etc.)
- o Group 4: Science (Biology, Chemistry, Physics, Computer Science and Environmental Science)
- o Group 5: Mathematics and Computer Science
- o Group 6: The Arts (Visual Arts, Dance, Music, Design technology or second subject from groups 2, 3, 4 and 5)

The IBDP curriculum is different from other curricula because:

- It encourages students to think critically and challenge what they are told.
- It is independent of governments and national systems and therefor able to incorporate best practice from a range of international frameworks and curricula.
- It encourages students to consider both, their local and international environment.
- Parents, who wish to send their children overseas for graduation, immediately after 12th standard level, usually prefer the IBDP. This is mainly because IBDP is recognised by number of universities worldwide, including in USA, Europe, Singapore, etc. As the IBDP curriculum is inquiry based, it develops self-learning, self-management, and creative skills in

students more effectively than traditional education methods can do. More information about IB Diploma can be found on the IB website[10].

□□□

---

[10] http://www.ibo.org

Section 2

Information about different career paths after 12th standard

- subject requirement and entrance test

3

Engineering:

Engineering is still the most sought-after career in our country. Every student seeking admission to an Engineering course, be it Bachelor of Technology (B. Tech.) or Bachelor of Engineering (B.E.) must appear for the stipulated entrance examination. The Indian Institute of Technology (IIT), and Birla Institute of Technology (BITS), are the most popular and nationally acclaimed institutes. Students seeking admission to the IITs have to appear for examinations conducted by the Central Board of Secondary Examination. Interested students first have to appear for Joint Engineering Examination Main (JEE Main)[11] test. Students coming in the top one and a half lakh ranks become eligible to appear for the Joint Engineering Examination Advanced (JEE Advanced) exam. From this, only about 7% students actually get admission in one of the 15 IITs in India. Thus getting into an IIT is very difficult, and only those who are extraordinarily brilliant and are ready to work really hard should give it a try; half-hearted attempts will almost never lead to success when it comes to cracking the JEE. More information about IIT entrance is available on the JEE website.

Other national level college, which is considered at par with the IIT, is the Birla Institute of Technology (BITS)[12] College,

---

[11] http://jeemain.nic.in
[12] http://www.bits-pilani.ac.in

which has campuses in Pilani, Goa, and Hyderabad. Admission to these colleges is given through the entrance exam - BITSAT conducted by BITS. More information about the different courses and admission procedure is available the BITS website.

The other nationally acclaimed engineering course is the B.Tech. course offered by Dhirubhai Ambani Institute of Information and Communication Technology[13], Gujrat. Admissions are given through the merit list of JEE Main. Another popular Engineering Institute is Vellore Institute of Technology (VIT). VIT conducts its own Engineering entrance exam called VITEEE. More information of the entrance exam and courses is available on VIT[14] website.

Maharashtra State Government conducts a single Common Entrance Test (MHT CET /MH CET) for all state-level Engineering, Pharmacy and Health Sciences courses. The test will have Physics (50 marks), Chemistry (50 marks), Mathematics (100 marks) and Biology (100 marks) papers. Those who wish to take admission in Engineering will have to appear for Physics, Chemistry and Mathematics papers. Admission will be based on the merit list drawn from the MH CET results. Detailed information about this test is available on the DTE[15] website.

There are around 300 Engineering colleges in Maharashtra offering around 1 lakh seats in almost 70 different specialties,

---

[13] http://www.daiict.ac.in
[14] http://vit.ac.in/
[15] http://www.dtemaharashtra.gov.in

apart from the traditional specialties; these are explained in Table No. 3.1 below.

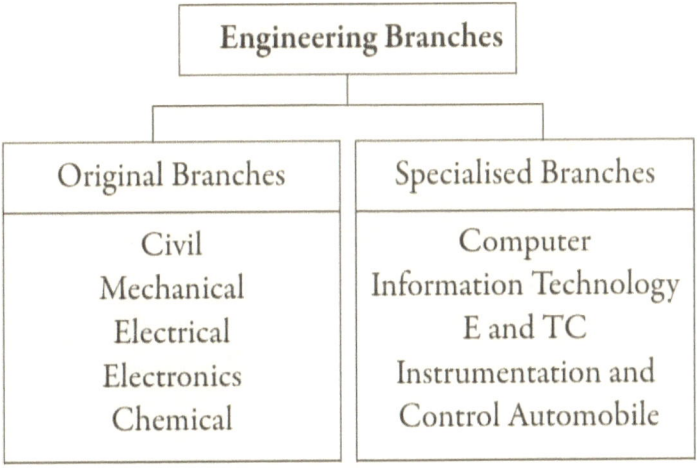

Chart: 3.1

Table No. 3.1

Mechanical	Civil	Chemical	Electrical
Aeronautics and Aerospace Engg.	Construction Engg.	Metallurgy and Material Science Engg.	Electrical Power and Machinery Engg.
Marine Engg.	Irrigation Engg.	Process Engg.	Electronics
Production Engg.	Structural Engg.	Molecular/Bim olecular Engg.	Communication and Control Engg.
	Transportation Engg.		Computer Engg.
	Environmental Engg.		
	Geotechnical Engg.		

*In addition to the Engineering courses in the IITs, State Engineering colleges etc., a 4-year **Bachelor of Technology (B.Tech.) in Agriculture Engineering** course is also offered, by the four Agriculture Universities in Maharashtra (discussed in the chapter "Careers in Agriculture").

Who should choose Engineering as a career?

- Those who have an aptitude for mathematics and science, and can apply higher level of knowledge.
- Those who can design a system or a component, and are good at analysis and interpretation of data.
- Those with inquisitive minds, who like to experiment new techniques.

Some more tips:

Before selecting a college, it is advisable to do research about the college – find out how many placements are done each year, the companies and their profiles that visit the college, the academic and personal profiles of the students who got the placements, etc. Interacting with the alumni of the college also can give an idea about whether the college is well suited to your needs.

4

Computer Science

Computer Science is the study of computers and computational systems. Computer scientists deal mostly with software and software systems; this includes their theory, design, development, and application.

Principal areas of study within Computer Science include:

- Artificial intelligence
- Computer systems and networks
- Network Security
- Database systems, database creation and management
- Human-computer interaction, vision and graphics,
- Numerical analysis
- Programming languages and software engineering (designing and writing programs for computers or other electronic devices)
- Design and analysis of algorithms to solve problem, and study the performance of computer hardware and software
- Machine learning: the study and construction of algorithms that can learn from, and make predictions on data.

It is a vast field and there is a constant need for different people having different skills. For example, software developers, data analysts, hardware technicians, web designers/developer, animators etc. Thus a career in

Computers may start from the engineering, science, or management side. In this section, we will get to know careers in computers that can take off form streams other than Engineering.

B.Sc. Computer Science

Those who wish to pursue a career in computer science, usually give first preference to engineering programs. But another way to enter the computer science field is to opt for the 3-year **Bachelor of Science, Computer Science** course. The main aim of this course is to develop the necessary skill set and analytical abilities for developing computer based solutions for real life problems. The curriculum consists of subjects like programming, database fundamentals, computer networks, system programming, web designing, data structures, databases, and preliminary software development. It also consists of Mathematics, Electronics and Statistics.

Admission to this course is given separately by each college and it's up to the respective college, whether it wants to conduct an entrance exam or not. Hence after you finish the 12th standard exam and other entrance tests, it's recommended that you find out the admission process for the college you are seeking admission into. Although not mandatory, students with a Master's degree in Computer Science have better prospects at being placed, than students who only have a Bachelor's degree.

Students who miss getting into a Computer Engineering course, B.Sc. Computer Science is another option for them to enter the field of the software apart of the Engineering course. It is a science oriented, highly academic course and has a great potential for research in the computer field.

Eligibility for admission to B.Sc. Computer Science is – 12th standard with English and any three Sciences (out of Physics, Chemistry, Biology, Mathematics, Geography); OR 3-year Diploma awarded by the Government Technical Institute or by the Board of Technical Education OR MCVC.

Who should choose Computer Science as a career?

- Learning computer science is a dynamic process; one has to be very agile all the time. Those who have very good numerical and reasoning ability, good cognition, and are able to apply knowledge in different scenarios can perform well in the computer science courses.

Career avenues after completing B.Sc. Computer Science:

- Programmer or Software Engineer
- Computer Scientist
- Logic Designer
- Systems Engineer, System integrator
- Systems Analyst
- System Administration
- Technical Support

Computer Science (CS) and Computer Engineering (CE)

Often students who want to pursue a career in computers want a clarification on what is the difference between computer science (CS) and computer engineering (CE). Both CS and CE study the use of the digital computers as a tool to facilitate modern technology. Although there is a substantial overlap, these two fields have different objectives. Below is a comparison of these fields.

Computer Science	Computer Engineering
Computer science is more about the theory of software, algorithms, data structures, networks, and databases etc. - More Mathematics based.	Computer Engineering deals with more hardware topics like embedded system design, electromagnetic compatibility, computer architecture, digital signal processing etc. - More Electrical - Electronics based
Advanced studies in CS contain specialised programming techniques and specific application domain	CE emphasises on solving problems in digital hardware and at the hardware-software interface
Focuses on "usability" – develop a software/program which enables the user to use the computer/an electronic device (laptops, smartphone, calculator etc.)	Focuses on "What makes up a computer?" - what goes in the device. They make computer parts work together
They are "Developers"	They are "Designers"
What do Computer Scientist do?: • Develop computer programs/software that makes the hardware work • Write CODE • Design Operating Systems that make the device work • They integrate the software with the hardware	What do Computer Engineers do?: • Design physical hardware that goes in the devices (Anything that has an electrical/electronic component, e.g. chips, processors etc. • Design systems • They design and build the hardware that supports a program

61

Computer Science	Computer Engineering
Example: • A computer engineer designs and develops a motherboard, processor, memory of a computer and computer scientist designs the operating system such as Windows Operating System that makes the computer usable • A computer engineer, working at Apple, designs the chips for the integrated circuits of the different components of the iPhone (e.g. memory, controls etc.) to work independently as well as with each other, while the computer scientist writes a program that makes all the applications in the iPhone run simultaneously.	

5

Computer Applications

The Bachelor of Computer Applications (BCA) course focuses on developing students to work in the field of computer applications in various business sectors. The BCA course equips to students with skill that can bridge the gap between the computer science and its applications. For example, a computer scientist develops a programming language and a computer applications professional, by using this language, develops a software, such as accounting packages, financial packages, database management software used by hospitals, hotels etc. which are used by the relevant users. The curriculum of BCA consists of computer application subjects like Computer Fundamentals and Office Automation, Database Concepts, Networking and Internet Programming, Multimedia Systems, Operating Systems and Programming Languages (like C++, Java, Visual Basic). Along with these subjects the curriculum also consists of subjects like Business Communication, Organisational Behaviour, Business Accounting, Cyber Law, and Cost Accounting, with an objective to make students ready to work in a business.

Eligibility: Students who have completed 12th standard years of education from any stream are eligible for admission to the 3-year **Bachelor of Computer Applications (BCA)** course is 12th standard from ANY stream. Although Mathematics is not mandatory, it is observed that, students who have studied Mathematics till 12th standard find it easier to understand the computer related subjects, and are able to grasp the concepts faster.

Similar to the B.Sc. Computer Science course, admission to this course is given separately by each college and it's up to the respective college, whether they want to conduct an entrance exam or not. Depending on their preference list, students should enquire about the admission procedure with the admission department of the respective college. Again, students who have a Master's in Computer Applications (MCA) degree have better prospects of landing a job; it is strongly advised to follow up the BCA course with the MCA course.

Difference between B.Sc. Computer Science and Bachelor of Computer Science:

Although both the courses are computer related, there is major different in the domains and objectives of these courses. Before selecting these courses, it is advisable to talk to alumni of both the courses and get an idea about what the courses deal with, what are the specific/general study skill-sets required, and whether the course is in-line with your aim and objectives. Here is a brief comparative idea about the same:

B.Sc. Computer Science	Bachelor of Computer Applications
Comes under the Faculty of Science. Entry through the science stream.	Comes under the Faculty of Commerce. Entry through ANY stream.
Approach is towards laying a foundation of Mathematical and Theory of computing (rather than teaching specific technologies that may quickly become obsolete).	Approach is towards introducing students to various areas of computer science, programming, and database designing, software engineering, networks and information systems.
Focus is on theoretical aspects and research, for example development of the programming languages like C, C++, Java, etc.	Focus is on diversified knowledge about computer applications like C++, financial accounting and management.
Learning scripting and coding	Learning on a specific piece of software or computer application such as graphics, financial accounting
More academic course, science oriented	More professional, designed according to the needs of IT Industry therefore application oriented
Companies hire B.Sc. Computer Science students as software testers, software developers, etc.	Organisations hire BCA students as per their requirement in a particular area which requires application of computer science principles and problem solving
E.g. - A computer scientist researches by using the knowledge of algorithms, mathematics, problem solving skills and develops the programming language like C++	The Computer Applications professional will use C++ to develop a computer game/healthcare package/financial software etc.

□□□

6

Information Technology

Information technology (IT) is the application of computers and telecommunications equipment to store, retrieve, transmit, and manipulate data, often in the context of a business or enterprise.

This term is commonly used as a synonym for computers and computer networks, but it also encompasses other information distribution technologies such as television and telephones. IT utilises existing operating systems, software, and applications to create an aggregated, larger system that solves a specific business problem. IT constructs a network from established building blocks to carry out a task, such as an automated supplies ordering service. IT students study network and database design in depth, and receive an introduction to basic theory and applied mathematics.

The size of the IT sector has increased by 35% per year in the last ten years and because of the increasing e-commerce businesses, social networking, internet banking etc., the field still has tremendous growth potential. Let us now understand few of the components of Information Technology is:

- Network: A computer network is a group of computers connected to each other electronically so that each computer can send and receive information to and from other computers it is connected to.

- Internet: The internet is a global network connecting millions of computers. When any two computers are connected to each other through internet, they can send and receive information/data such as text, graphics, voice, video, and even computer programs.
- No single person/organisation/country owns the internet. It's more of a concept than an actual tangible entity.

Education:

One can break into the field of Information Technology through different routes, and various certificate and degree courses:

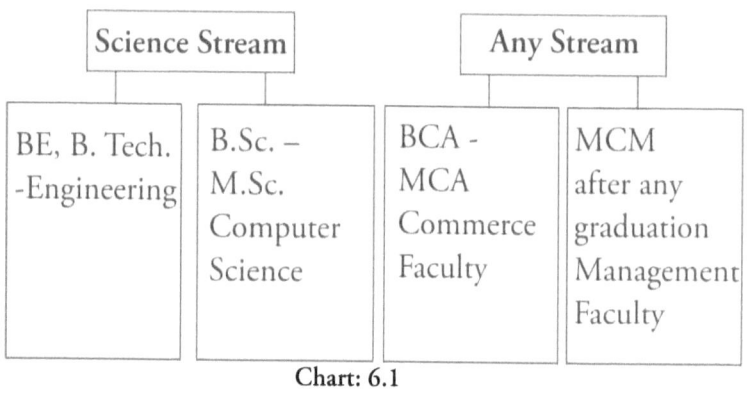

Chart: 6.1

Eligibility criteria for Engineering, B.Sc. and BCA have been discussed previously in this chapter.

MCM (Master of Computer Management): This is a 2-year postgraduate course. The objective of this course is to develop knowledge and skills required to plan, design and build complex application software systems applicable in all industry sectors including business, health, education, and services. Graduates from any faculty are eligible for this course.

Directorate of Technical Education, Government of Maharashtra conducts a Common Entrance Test (MAH-MCA-CET) generally in the month of February every year.

Certificate Courses: There are different types of certificate courses from which to choose, according to the objective of the learner.

Undergraduate level Certifications:

MS-CIT - This is an Information Technology literacy course started by Maharashtra Knowledge Corporation Ltd. (MKCL). Eligibility for this course is 10th standard. This course covers Computer Basics like personalizing desktop, files and folder management, using computer accessories like paint, wordpad, notepad, windows media player etc. along with troubleshooting.

- **The Microsoft Certified Solutions Engineer (MCSE) Certification**: Microsoft offers a wide range of online certification programs designed to develop IT skills. These certifications are available in different areas such as Server (Windows Server, Exchange Server, Lync, etc.), Desktop (Windows, devices), Applications (Office, Office 365, Microsoft Dynamics), Database (SQL Server), Developer (Visual Studio, Share Point Application, Microsoft Azure). This certification is often a starting point for more advanced and specialised certifications. Minimum qualification required for this certification is 12th standard pass.

- **Certificate in Computer Basics and Multilingual Technology by C-DAC**: This is a 45-day course (total course hours – 36). It focuses on computer fundamentals; give introduction to multilingual word processing application, and an overview of the tremendous advantages of the Internet. Students who are interested in understanding computers and their utility should join this course.

Graduate Level Certifications:

- Those who are looking at computers and IT as a career path should opt for these courses. CCNA, CCNP, CCIE, Ethical Hacking are examples of such certifications. Minimum qualification for these courses is graduation. Many such courses are offered by Centre for Development of Advanced Computing, Pune (C-DAC)[16].

Indian Institute of Information Technology (IIIT):

Indian Institutes of Information Technology (IIIT) are Deemed Universities established by Institutes under Ministry of Human Resource Development, Government of India. **Deemed university**, or **Deemed-to-be-University**, is an autonomous university recognised by the Universities Grant Commission (UGC). The autonomous status is granted by the Department of Higher Education, MHRD[17].

Similar to the IIT's, IIM's, ISI's, IISER's and IISc, IIITs also enjoy a special status as Institutes of National Importance under the Indian Institute of Information Technology Act. Currently there are four IIITs funded by the MHRD, and 16 IIITs operate under Public Private Partnership (PPP) mode.

---

[16] http://www.cdac.in
[17] http://mhrd.gov.in/iiits

Details of these institutes are available at http://mhrd.gov.in/iiits

Courses: The IIITs offer undergraduate (B.Tech.) and graduate (M.Tech. and MBA) degree in Information Technology, Computer Engineering, Design, Mechanical Design, etc. Many of the IIITs offer a 5-year Integrated Master's degree and a Ph.D. as well.

Admission: Admission is given through the merit list of JEE Main results.

Table 6.1

MHRD Funded IIITs		
1	ABV -Indian Institute of Information Technology and Management, Gwalior	http://www.iiitm.ac.in
2	Indian Institute of Information Technology (IIIT), Allahabad	http://www.iiita.ac.in/
3	Indian Institute of Information Technology, Design and Manufacturing (IIITDM), Chennai	http://www.iiitdm.ac.in/
4	Pandit Dwarka Prasad Mishra Indian Institute of Information Technology, Design and Manufacturing (IIITDM), Jabalpur	http://www.iiitdmj.ac.in

Table 6.2

IIITs in PPP Mode			
1	IIIT, Chittoor, Andhra Pradesh	9	IIIT, Senapati, Manipur
2	IIIT, Guwahati	10	IIIT, Lucknow, Uttar Pradesh
3	IIIT, Kalyani, West Bengal	11	IIIT, Kottayam, Kerala
4	IIIT, Una, Himachal Pradesh	12	IIIT, Dharward, Karnataka
5	IIIT, Vadodara Gujarat	13	IIIT, Pune, Maharashtra
6	IIIT, Kota, Rajasthan	14	IIIT, Bhopal, Madhya Pradesh
7	IIIT, Tiruchirappalli, Tamil Nadu	15	IIIT, Bodhjungnagar, Tripura
8	IIIT, Sonepat, Haryana	16	IIIT, Kakinada, Andhra Pradesh

Career avenues in Information Technology:

- Computer Networks
- Software Development and Programming
- Systems Analyst
- Data Processing
- Software Developer/Programmer
- Database Administrator
- Systems and Network Administrator
- Web Designer/Developer
- Multimedia Programmer
- Software Testing
- Technical Writer

7

Computer Animation

Those who are good in design skills, and wish to study a course that will integrate design and computer graphics, can think of doing the 3-year **Bachelor of Science (B.Sc.) Computer Animation** course. The objective of this course is to develop competencies and skills needed for becoming an effective animator. The curriculum consists of subjects like 2D and 3D Animation, Introduction to Programming Languages, Multimedia, Productions Process, Sketching, and Landscaping.

The requirement of this course is similar to that of the B.Sc. Computer Science Course. Intermediate/Elementary drawing exam certificates are desirable.

Who should do Computer Animation?

This is a very creative course. The student needs to develop a concept, and then create 2D and/or 3D animations using computer graphics, applying his/her imagination. Hence the most important abilities/skills would be a good aesthetic sense, vivid imagination, acute observation, and good cognition. Those who can create stories and tell them effectively can think of this career.

8

Commercial Pilot (Civil Aviation)

Civil Aviation is concerned with all activities involving the operation of an aircraft, for civilian purposes. There are various careers in civil aviation and one of the most sought after is that of a Pilot. Other popular occupations are - Aircrew, Air Traffic Management and other Technical aspects of the aircraft.

How to become a commercial pilot:

In the last decade, various domestic and international airlines have sprung up in the private sector. Because of this, Commercial Pilot has become a very attractive career possibility. There are many Directorate General of Civil Aviation (DGCA)[18] approved training schools, which offer the commercial pilot training; the DGCA is an attached office of the Ministry of Civil Aviation.

Indira Gandhi Rashtriya Uran Akademi (IGRUA)[19], Fursatganj, Raibareli, is the pilot training school in our country which is run by the Ministry of Civil Aviation, Government of India. It has state-of-the-art technology and facilities required for pilot training, including 21 aircrafts of its own, and a 1.5km runway. This academy offers a 15-month training to become a commercial pilot. Those who have passed 12th standard with English, Physics, and Mathematics are eligible to appear for the

---

[18] http://dgca.nic.in
[19] http://igrua.gov.in

national level entrance exam. Those who get selected from the entrance test, have to appear for the pilot battery (aptitude) test. The final step in the selection procedure is an interview, conducted on campus at Raibareli. More information is available on the website of Indira Gandhi Rashtriya Uran Akademi.[20]

Apart from IGRUA, there are around 40 other pilot training approved schools all over India. Information about them is available on the DGCA website.

To become a commercial pilot from other flying clubs, there are three stages:

- **Student Pilot Licence (SPL):** Consists of a written, objective type test; eligibility for the test is 10th standard pass, and age limit is 16 years.
- **Private Pilot Licence (PPL):** Consists of practical and theory examination. Practical aspect of the course consists of 40 hours of flying with instructor and 20 hours of solo flying. The theory paper is conducted by DGCA. The training period is nearly two years.
- **Commercial Pilot Licence (CPL):** Consists of about 250 solo flying hours, including the 60 hours of PPL. Along with the theory exam, there is also a Fitness test. After clearing all tests, the licence is issued.

Being a pilot is a tough job. One has to be disciplined, patient, responsible, punctual, committed, and confident. This profession requires lot of hard work; there is no cutting slack. One has to be on his/her toes, always alertness, and away from

---

[20] http://igrua.gov.in

home and family a lot. This is one of the few professions that require its individuals to be mentally, emotionally, and physically fit. Students considering it as a career option should be prepared to put in that kind of hard work and dedication.

9

Merchant Navy

Sea transport has historically been the largest carrier of freight. At one point in time, the sea was the only way for people to travel to foreign lands. With the advent of aviation, the importance of the sea and ships as a mode of transport has significantly reduced. However, it is still favoured for short leisurely trips and pleasure cruises. Merchant Navy provides a major mode of transport international cargo including oil, minerals, food, machinery etc. in different parts of world. It is the backbone of the world economy.

Right from the Captain of the ship to an engineer in the machine room of the ship, to the deck crew, the cooks and helpers in the kitchen, and even shore-jobs – the Merchant Navy offers a wide-range of jobs for people with different educational qualifications or skills.

Those who wish to pursue a maritime career should be mentally prepared to stay away from home and family at a stretch, lasting typically 3 months or more. However, for those prepared to do that, a career in merchant navy can prove to be very lucrative. It also offers the opportunity to travel all around the world. It can prove to be an exceptionally gratifying career, especially for those who like to take on challenges.

There are various undergraduate and postgraduate programs that one can opt for, providing different routes to enter the field. All these courses are conducted by the Indian Maritime University (IMU)[21]. This is a teaching and affiliating university under the Ministry of Defence, Government of India, established by the Act of parliament in 2008. This university is responsible for conducting all types of exam including the entrance test of the graduate programs. The undergraduate programs are offered by three different schools under the university:

- School of Nautical Studies
- School of Marine Engineering
- School of Naval Architecture and Naval Engineering

The table below gives an overview of the different undergraduate programs conducted by these schools under the university:

---

[21] http://www.imu.edu.in/

Table 9.1

School of Nautical Sciences - Program in Nautical and Maritime Science		
Program	Eligibility	Location
1-year pre-sea training diploma in Nautical Science leading to B.Sc. (Applied Nautical Science) + 18-month on board training after one year + 4-month Functions Course + Appear for Second Mates Examination leading to B.Sc. Degree	• 12th standard pass with PCM and English with 60% + **Entrance Test** OR • B.Sc. (PCM) or B.Sc.(Electronics) with 50% marks OR • B.E./B. Tech from IIT or AICT recognised Engineering College	Chennai Mumbai Cochin
3-year B.Sc. (Nautical Science)	• 12th standard pass with PCM and English with 60% + **Entrance Test**	Chennai Mumbai Kolkata
3-year B.Sc. (Maritime Science)	• 12th standard pass with PCM & English with 60% + **Entrance Test**	Mumbai

Table 9.2

School of Marine Engineering - Program in Marine Engineering		
Program	Eligibility	Location
4-year B. Tech. Marine Engineering OR Lateral Entry into second year engineering after Engineering Diploma in Marine/Mechanical Engineering	• 12th standard pass with PCM & English with 60% + **Entrance Test**	Chennai Mumbai Kolkata

Table 9.3

School of Naval Architecture and Ocean Engineering - Program in Nautical and Maritime Science		
Program	Eligibility	Location
3-year B.Sc.(Ship Building and Repair)	• 12ᵗʰ standard pass with PCM & English with 60% + **Entrance Test** OR • B.Sc. (PCM) or B.Sc.(Electronics) with 50% marks OR • B.E. / B.Tech from IIT or AICT recognised Engineering College	Vishakha patnam
4-year B. Tech. (Naval Architecture and Ocean Engineering) OR Lateral entry into second year engineering after Diploma in Shipbuilding Technology, Goa or B.Sc.(Ship Building and Repair)	• 12ᵗʰ standard pass with PCM and English with 60% + **Entrance Test**	Visakhap atnam

These courses are offered in the University's campuses at different places in India:

IMU Mumbai Campus:

- The Training Ship Chanakya
- Lal Bahadur College of Advanced Maritime Studies and Research
- The Marine Engineering and Research Institute (MERI)

IMU Visakhapatnam Campus:

- Indian Maritime University Visakhapatnam Campus (Formerly known as National Ship Design Research Centre)

IMU Kolkata Campus:

- Marine Engineering and Research Institute (MERI)
- Indian Institute of Port Management (IIPM)

IMU Chennai Campus:

- Indian Maritime University Chennai Campus

IMU Cochin Campus:

- Indian Maritime University Cochin Campus

Apart from the Government Institutes, there are many private institutes recognised by the Directorate General of Shipping (D.G. Shipping)[22]. Information of these institutes is available on D.G. Shipping website.

❑❑❑

---

[22]  http://dgshipping.gov.in

10

Health Sciences

Entry to ANY course in Health Sciences begins with the PCB group in 11th and 12th standard. There are many courses in Health Sciences. In addition to the traditional courses like Medicine, Dentistry, Ayurveda, Physiotherapy, or Nursing, there are a number of paramedical graduate courses offered by Government-aided, as well as private colleges affiliated to the Maharashtra University of Health Sciences (MUHS)[23], Nashik, and the Deemed Universities. The tables below give a list of different courses offered in the Health Sciences stream.

Table 10.1

#	Course Name	Degree	Admission Requirement
1	Bachelor of Medicine and Surgery	M.B.B.S.	
2	Bachelor of Dental Surgery	B.D.S.	
3	Bachelor of Ayurvedic Medicine and Surgery	B.A.M.S.	• 12th Science with PCB + Entrance Test
4	Bachelor of Homeopathic Medicine and Surgery	B.H.M.S.	
5	Bachelor of Unani Medicine and Surgery	B.U.M.S.	• *BASLP- 12th std+PC+B/M/CS

---

[23] http://www.muhs.ac.in

#	Course Name	Degree	Admission Requirement
6	Bachelor of Physiotherapy	B.P.Th.	• BP&O - 12ᵗʰ std+PC+B/M
7	Bachelor of Occupational Therapy	B.O.Th.	
8	Bachelor of Audiology and Speech, Language Pathology	B.A.S.L.P.	
9	Bachelor of Prosthetics	B.P.& O.	
10	B.Sc. Nursing	B.Sc. Nursing	

P=Physics,   C=Chemistry,   B=Biology,   M=Mathematics, CS=Computer Science

Admissions to Health Science Courses:

1. Entrance Tests in Maharashtra:

In, Maharashtra the admissions to Medical, Dental, Ayurved, Unani, Physiotherapy, Occupational Therapy, Nursing (B.Sc.) are allotted through the Maharashtra State Common Entrance Test (MHT-CET) conducted by the Government of Maharashtra.

Eligibility to the entrance test is 12ᵗʰ standard pass with Physics, Chemistry and Biology. MHT-CET 2016 is applicable for admissions to MBBS, BDS, BAMS, BHMS, BUMS, BPTh, BOTh, BASLP, BP&O, B.Sc. [Nursing] in all Government, Municipal Corporation and Private aided, Unaided & Minority Health Science Institution/Colleges.

More information is available on the website of Directorate of Medical Education & Research (DMER)[24].

Association of Management of Unaided Private Medical and Dental Colleges (AMUPMDC)[25], Maharashtra conducts a separate Asso-CET for admissions to private, unaided colleges. Conduction of Asso-CET is subject to change according to the Government Rules. Eligibility criteria to appear for this exam are the same as that for MHT-CET.

In addition to these tests, there are some deemed Universities offering courses in Health Sciences; these Universities conduct their own entrance examination and are not bound to admit students through MHT-CET. The eligibility criteria for these too, is the same as that for MHT-CET. Interested students need to appear for the entrance tests for each Deemed University, separately.

2. All India Pre-Medical/Pre-Dental Test:

The All India level Pre-medical and pre-dental test (AIPMT)[26] is conducted every year in the month of May by the Central Board of Secondary Education, Delhi. Fifteen per cent of the seats in all government medical and dental colleges of the participating states (all states except Andhra Pradesh, Telangana and Jammu & Kashmir) are filled through this test. The main eligibility criteria are 12th standard pass with English, Physics, Chemistry and Biology/Biotechnology.

---

[24] http://www.dmer.org
[25] http://www.amupmdc.org
[26] http://aipmt.nic.in

3. Armed Forces Medical College:

The Armed Forces Medical College (AFMC), is India's premier medical college, and provides training to under-graduate and post-graduate medical and nursing students with assured career prospects in the defence services. (More information about this is given in the Chapter on "Defences".)

4. Other Medical Entrance Tests:

There are other renowned medical institutes all over India, which conduct their entrance tests at the national level. Information about these entrance tests can be found from the websites listed below:

1) All India Institute of Medical Sciences (AIIMS)[27]
2) Christian Medical College Ludhiana (CMC-Ludhiana)[28]
3) Christian Medical College Vellore (CMC-Vellore)[29]
4) Jawaharlal Institute of Postgraduate Medical Education & Research (JIPMER)[30]
5) Mahatma Gandhi Institute of Medical Sciences (MGIMS), Sewagram[31]

Note: Common Entrance test for MBBS and BDS courses all over India

In April 2016 the Supreme Court directed the Government and the Central Board of Secondary Education (CBSE) to

---

[27] http://www.aiims.edu/en.html
[28] http://cmcludhiana.in
[29] http://www.cmch-vellore.edu
[30] http://jipmer.edu.in/
[31] https://www.mgims.ac.in

conduct a single common entrance test for Medical (MBBS), Dental (BDS) and Post Graduate courses. The test is called 'National Eligibility Entrance Test' (NEET). Thus henceforth there will be a SINGLE entrance examination for all MBBS and BDS courses, all over the country.

This is will decrease the burden of appearing for multiple entrance exams (mentioned above) in a substantial way and make the lives of the students quite simpler. For details please check the websites of Medical Council of India (MCI) and that of All India Pre-Medical and Pre-Dental Test (AIPMT).

Admissions for the other Health Science Courses in Maharashtra State will most probably be continued through MHT-CET. Students are advised to find out thorough information from authorized sources like Directorate of Medical Education and Research (DMER) and keep an update of current news from the leading newspapers and then make an informed decision.

Paramedical:

A Paramedic is an expert who assists doctors in their specialised areas and facilities for better diagnosis, treatment, and therapy; paramedics form the backbone of medical services. Paramedical training enables one to become an expert technician in a specific area, for example spinal injury management, obstetrics, fracture management, etc. A variety of 3-year Bachelor's Courses in Paramedical Technology have been started, taking into consideration the pivotal role that paramedics play in medical services. The courses in Maharashtra are affiliated to MUHS.

Eligibility criteria: 12th standard pass with Physics, Chemistry and Biology. There is no entrance test or a centralised admission process. The student has to submit the required documents to different colleges independently. The colleges then admit the students on the basis of a merit list, drawn taking all applications into account. Below is the list of the different 3-year Bachelor of Paramedical Technology (B.P.M.T.).

List of currently offered courses:

1. BPMT-Blood Transfusion
2. BPMT-Optometry
3. BPMT-Cardiology Technician
4. BPMT-Community Medicine
5. BPMT-Endoscopy
6. BPMT-Laboratory Technician
7. BPMT-Neurology Technician
8. BPMT-Perfusion Technician
9. BPMT-Radiography
10. BPMT-OT Technician
11. BPMT-Emergency/General Medicine
12. BPMT-Forensic Science
13. BPMT-Emergency Med. Service
14. BPMT-Anaesthesia
15. BPMT-Cyto
16. BPMT-Histopathology
17. BPMT-Plaster
18. BPMT-Clinical Psychologist
19. BPMT-Transfusion Medicine
20. BPMT-Transfusion Medicine

11

Veterinary Science

Veterinary Science deals with diagnosis, treatment, and management of animals and birds. The basic principle of studying veterinary science is similar to that of human medicine covered in the medical, ayurvedic, or homeopathy courses; it includes subjects like physiology, anatomy, treatment and prevention of diseases, etc. But the job profile of a veterinary doctor is much different from that of an M.B.B.S. doctor; while doctors are not concerned with 'reproduction', a veterinary doctor's job also includes animal breeding (animal husbandry) and handling of livestock.

In addition to prevention and treatment of diseases, veterinary doctors – or 'vets' – perform surgeries as well. Animal husbandry, which is a major part of veterinary sciences, includes research and development of improved breeds, animal vaccinations, research on preventing diseases that are transmitted by animals, poultry management, wildlife conservation, and many other aspects of animals. In short, a veterinary doctor plays a major role in the conservation of livestock and domestic animals. Animals in different aspects – domestic pets, livestock, animals in the zoo, laboratories, poultry, animal husbandry departments – are looked after by the vets.

Veterinary Science and Animal Husbandry Graduates can work in the Central and State government owned dairy and poultry farms. They can also work for pharmaceutical manufacturers, armed forces, and insurance companies. They can also start their private veterinary practice after graduation. Finally, they may consider going abroad and furthering their knowledge and/or skills.

Bachelor of Veterinary Science and Animal Husbandry (B.V.Sc. and A.H.):

Duration of this course varies from either 5 years or Four and a half years. A six-month internship is inclusive of the course. There are national and state level veterinary colleges in India. The Veterinary Council of India (VCI)[32] is a statutory body, established under Ministry of Agriculture, Government of India.

The Maharashtra Animal & Fishery Sciences University (MAFSU)[33], which is the state university in Maharashtra, runs various bachelor, master and doctoral level programs in Veterinary Science & Animal Husbandry as well as in Dairy Technology and Fishery Science in affiliated colleges in Maharashtra state.

Veterinary Colleges

1   Bombay Veterinary College, Mumbai (BVC)
2   Nagpur Veterinary College, Mumbai (NVC)
3   College of Veterinary and Animal Sciences, Parbhani (COVAS)

---

[32] http://www.vci.nic.in
[33] http://www.mafsu.in

4   College of Veterinary and Animal Sciences, Udgir (COVAS)

5   Krantisinh Nana Patil College of Veterinary Science, Shirwal, Satara (KNPCVS)

6   Post Graduate Institute of Veterinary and Animal Sciences, Akola (PGIVAS)

Fishery Science Colleges

1   College of Fishery Science, Telangkhedi, Nagpur (CFS)

2   College of Fishery Science, Udgir

Dairy Technology Colleges

1   College of Dairy Technology, Warud, Pusad (CDT)
2   College of Dairy Technology, Udgir, Latur (CDT)

Each of these colleges has some highly specialized and well developed departments which include India's first Veterinary Nuclear Medicine Center (VNMC) at Mumbai, Embryo Transfer Technology Laboratory and Mineral & Hormonal Assay Laboratory at Akola, Swine Fever Surveillance Center at Nagpur etc.

The same MHT-CET, conducted for admissions to courses of health sciences field, is used to conduct admissions to state level veterinary colleges; the demarcation between the two fields is maintained by narrowing the choice of colleges available: those interested in the Veterinary colleges are not eligible to apply to the Health Sciences Course, and vice-versa. Eligibility to appear for the test is hence the same. Information for this can be found on DMER website.

The **All India Pre-Veterinary Test (AIPVT)** is conducted by the Veterinary Council of India, in April/May. Candidates appearing for the 12th standard exam with Physics, Chemistry, and Biology are eligible to appear for this exam. 15% of the total number of seats of all veterinary colleges in the state level colleges is allotted to students selected through this test. More information about this is available on the website of Veterinary Council of India[34].

---

[34] http://www.vci.nic.in

12

Pharmacy

Pharmacy is the science and technique of preparing and dispensing drugs; it is a rapidly growing sector with a lot of career prospects. Pharmaceutical sciences are a group of interdisciplinary areas of study concerned with the design, action, delivery, and disposition of drugs. They apply knowledge from chemistry (inorganic, physical, biochemical, and analytical), biology (anatomy, physiology, biochemistry, cell biology, and molecular biology), epidemiology, statistics, mathematics, physics, and chemical engineering.

Note: While somewhat closely related, the studies of pharmacy and pharmacology are unique on their own. In the Indian context, a pharmacologist is a doctor. The pathway to become a pharmacologist begins with an undergraduate degree in medicine and a post-graduation in Pharmacology afterwards. The table below gives an idea about the difference between these two fields:

Those who study Pharmacology	Those who study Pharmacy
They are health professionals.	They are scientists
They Study effects of drugs on human body and appropriate drug administration according to patient's complaint. Prescribe drugs as per the patient's requirement	They study how to synthesize, purify, identify and analyse medicinal agents. They also study marketing, distribution of selling of medicines.

In short, they study what a drug does to a body or what a body does to a drug	They will research a new drug and give it to the health professionals to use and give feedback.
They are concerned with patients' health and wellness	They are concerned with developing and researching medications in healthcare
Thy study how drugs affect cellular systems through molecular, biological and physiological effects and then analyse the absorption, delivery and excretion of the drugs from the system.	They mainly deal with the end products of a pharmaceutical industry for e.g. mixing, granulation, compression, coating etc. of drugs

Career opportunities in the pharmaceutical industry range from those in sales and marketing, to research and development, to management. The various areas where a pharmacist can find career opportunities are:

- Manufacturing
- Sales and Marketing
- Quality Control
- Pharmaceutical Research
- Hospital Pharmacy or self-owned Pharmacy (shop)
- Chemical Industry
- Food and drug control organisations
- Cosmetic Industry
- Pharmaceutical Management
- And many others…

There are three options available in Pharmacy:
- **Diploma in Pharmacy (D. Pharm.):** a 3-year course after 12th standard; career options after completing the

course are – set up your own pharmaceutical shop, hospital pharmacy or Medical representative

- **Bachelor's Degree in Pharmacy (B. Pharm.)**: a 4-year degree course after 12th standard.
- **Doctor of Pharmacy (Pharma-D)**: a 6-year integrated course after 12th standard.

Admission:

There are over a hundred aided and unaided pharmacy colleges in Maharashtra. Admissions are given on merit in the Maharashtra State Common entrance Test: MT-CET, conducted by the Directorate of Technical Education (DTE)[35]. Eligibility criteria for the entrance test is: 12th standard with English + Physics + Chemistry + (Biology / Mathematics / Biotechnology / Technical Vocational Subject)

Other National Level Courses in Pharmacy:

- **IIT - Banaras Hindu University**[36] offers a 4-year Bachelor's Degree (B.Pharm.) and 5-year Integrated Dual Degree (M.Pharm) course. Admission through JEE Main.
- **Birla Institute of Technology**[37] has campuses at Pilani and Hyderabad, and offers a 4-year B.Pharm course - Eligibility criteria for their entrance test BITS Admission Test (BITSAT) are: 12th standard with Physics + Chemistry + (Biology/Mathematics).

❑❑❑

---

[35] http://www.dtemaharashtra.gov.in
[36] http://www.iitbhu.ac.in
[37] http://www.bits-pilani.ac.in

13

Agricultural Science

Agriculture is the science of cultivating the soil, harvesting crops, and raising livestock. Agriculture includes production, cultivation, growing, and harvesting of any agricultural or horticultural product, raising of livestock or poultry, or any other task that concerns with farming.

India is among the largest producers of vegetables and fruits in the world and has an equally strong floriculture base; our country is one of the greatest exporters of agricultural commodities; right from fruits (like mangos, oranges, pomegranates) to mushrooms, spices, vegetables, oilseeds, cereals, and flowers, a number of agricultural products are exported in huge quantities every year. Agricultural exports are getting a good support from the government as well and hence the large business houses also getting interested in this business. Because of this, various job opportunities are available and substantial school is available for entrepreneurship.

Education:

Education in Agricultural Science is governed and coordinated by the Indian Council of Agricultural Research (ICAR), an autonomous body under the Department of Agricultural Research and Education, Ministry of Agriculture. ICAR conducts the ICAR All India Entrance Examination

(ICAR - AIEEA)[38] for the Bachelor and Masters courses in Agricultural Science. All the Agricultural State Universities allot 15% undergraduate and postgraduate seats through this examination. Candidates who are selected through AIEEA entrance exam are also awarded National Talent Scholarship in Agriculture and Allied Sciences. More information can be found on ICAR-AIEEA website.

Agriculture Universities in Maharashtra:

There are 4 Agriculture Universities in Maharashtra offering 10 undergraduate courses of 4-year duration:

    i.   Mahatma Phule Krishi Vidyapeeth, Rahuri, Dist. Ahmednagar

    ii.   Dr. Panjabrao Deshmukh Krishi Vidyapeeth, Akola

    iii.   Vasantrao Naik Marathwada Krishi Vidyapeeth, Parbhani

    iv.   Dr. Balasaheb Sawant Konkan Krishi Vidyapeeth, Dapoli, Dist. Ratnagiri

---

[38] http://icarexam.net

Table 13.1

#	Course	Eligibility
1	B.Sc. Agriculture	12th standard with English + Physics + Chemistry + Biology; OR Agriculture Diploma (*Mathematics is not compulsory but those who haven't done Math, need to complete deficiency courses as prescribed by the University.)
2	B.Sc. Horticulture	
3	B.Sc. Forestry	
4	B.Sc. Agriculture Biotechnology	
5	B.Sc. Fisheries	
6	B.Sc. Animal Husbandry	
7	B.Tech. Food Technology	
8	B.Tech. Agriculture Engineering	12th standard with English + Physics + Chemistry + Mathematics
9	B.Sc. (Hons.) Home Science	12th standard in (Arts/Science/Commerce) + English
10	B.B.A. Agriculture	10+2 with English+Physics+Chemistry+Biology+ Mathematics *Those who haven't done Math or Bio, need to complete deficiency courses as prescribed by the University

There is no entrance test for admissions to the Agriculture degree courses in the state universities. Admissions are given on the basis of marks obtained in 12ᵗʰ standard exam. Children of farmers or those who had NCC or Agriculture as one of the subjects in 12ᵗʰ standard, get an advantage in terms of bonus marks. The admissions are given through the Maharashtra Council for Agriculture Education and Research (MCAER)[39]. Detailed information can be found on MCAER website.

Diploma in Agriculture: The unaided agricultural colleges in Maharashtra offer a 3-year Diploma in Agriculture after 10ᵗʰ standard. Students completing the diploma will be eligible for the 4-year B.Sc. Agriculture course and will get a lateral entry in the second year of the course.

❑❑❑

---

[39] http://www.mcaer.org/

14

Biotechnology

'Bio' means life and 'Technology' is defined as application of science for a specific purpose. Thus Biotechnology is the use of living systems and organisms to develop or make products. It is an interdisciplinary science which not only includes Biology, but also Mathematics, Physics, and Chemistry. The application of Biotechnology ranges from agriculture, medicine, nutrition, genetics, microbiology, environmental conservation, animal sciences etc. to various industries like food, pharmaceutical, chemical, bio-products, textiles etc. These applications can be grouped under three broad categories: Medical, Environmental, and Industrial Biotechnology.

Medical Biotechnology is responsible for research and development of new drugs, vaccines, pharmaceutical recombinant proteins like insulin, and diagnostic products that help in treatment and prevention of human diseases. Applications of Medical Biotechnology are:

- Genetic Engineering is the process of the deliberate modification of the characteristics of an organism by manually adding new DNA into it with a goal to add one or more new traits that were not present earlier. Examples of genetically engineered (transgenic) organisms include plants which are resistant to some insects, plants that can tolerate herbicides, and crops with modified oil content.

- Pharmacology – Production of genetically engineered drugs. For e.g. Human insulin was first produced in Escherichia Coli through recombinant DNA technology.
- Production of monoclonal antibodies – Antibodies (specific proteins that target pathogens invading our body) that are clones of a parent cell.
- Stem Cell research and storage – Embryonic stem cell are collected and stored for further use in case of any damage to the body.

Environmental Biotechnology addresses ecological issues like waste gas and wastewater management, composting, hazardous soil-pollutants, bio-magnification, and other, and seeks to find solutions to the same using microbes. For example, Soil Bio-Treatment makes use of bacteria to degrade soil contaminants.

Industrial/White Biotechnology uses micro-organisms, or their enzymes, to make bio-based products such as food and feed, paper and pulp, textiles, chemicals, detergents, and bioenergy (such as biofuels or biogas).

The major scope for Biotechnology is in research as it is a developing field. Biotechnologists can find careers in government supported or private entities such as universities, research institutes, chemical industries, agricultural companies, aquaculture, food manufacturers, and with pharmaceutical industries as research scientists/assistants. They can be employed in the areas of planning, production, and management of bioprocessing industries. In short, the scope to develop a career in the field of biotechnology is wide and ranges from life sciences to industry and further to agriculture.

Who should go for Biotechnology?

Those who have a research aptitude - inquisitiveness, patience, perseverance, can concentrate for long hours, an inclination towards looking at minute details, and methodical approach. Students aspiring to make a career in biotechnology should also possess good problem solving, and analysing skills.

Education:

Better career opportunity in this field is generally possible at the postgraduate level, and because it is a research-oriented field, a PhD is advisable. Although there are many undergraduate (B.Sc. Biotechnology) courses available, students possessing a B.Sc. degree in Botany, Zoology, Microbiology, Virology, Medicine, Chemistry, Physics, or Agriculture can also do well in Biotechnology, provided they take at least a Masters or a PhD Students from Engineering background can also pursue a career in Biotechnology. Some IITs have a 4-year B. Tech or an integrated B. Tech-M. Tech course in Biotechnology. The list below gives an idea of the different pathways one can choose to enter the field of Biotechnology:

- B.Sc. in Biotechnology
- B.Sc. in other Sciences
- B.Tech in Biotechnology
- Integrated M.Sc. in Biotechnology
- Integrated M.Tech. in Biotechnology
- B.Sc. Agriculture/Agriculture Biotechnology
- Bachelor of Veterinary Science
- M.B.B.S.
- B.Tech/B.E. Biomedical Engineering

100

B.Sc. Biotechnology: To enrol into a 3-year B.Sc. Biotechnology course, the minimum requirement is, 12th standard with English and Biology, and any two of the following subjects: Physics, Chemistry, Mathematics or Biotechnology. Admissions to this course are given separately by each college, and it's up to these colleges, whether they want to conduct an entrance exam. Hence it is important to find out about the admission process in each college separately.

In addition to the B.Sc. Biotechnology course there are a few national level integrated courses, at the end of which the student is awarded with Master's degree in Biotechnology – either a M.Sc. or M.Tech; typically, these courses last 5 or 6 years.

5-year Integrated M.Sc./6-year Integrated M.Tech in University of Pune:

- The Institute of Bioinformatics and Biotechnology (I.B.B.) of Pune University offers a nationally acclaimed, 5-year integrated M.Sc. in Biotechnology course.

- The main objective of the course is to provide balanced and comprehensive knowledge of basic and applied sciences related to Biotechnology that would enhance the basic aptitude of each student and prepare them to take up the challenges in the varied and multi-faceted applications of Biotechnology.

- Students are offered the option to continue for 6th year, which would make them eligible for M.Tech (Biotechnology) degree, or to opt out of it, accepting a Master's (M.Sc.) degree instead. The sixth year focuses on significant industry/research project component in addition to related courses.

- The admission is given through a separate national level entrance test conducted by the department.
- Eligibility for the entrance exam is 12th standard in Science.
- There are only 30 seats available nationally for this course.

In addition to this course some IITs also offer graduate course in Biotechnology. The table below gives an overview of these courses:

Table 14.1

#	Institute	Course	Admission
1	IIT Delhi[40]	Dual Degree - B.Tech. in Biochemical Engineering and Biotechnology, and M. Tech. in Biochemical Engineering and Biotechnology (http://www.iitd.ac.in)	Through JEE Main and JEE Advance
2	IIT Kharagpur [41]	4-year B. Tech. in Biotechnology and Biomedical Engineering	
3		5-year Dual Degree B.Tech - M.Tech in Biotechnology and Biomedical	

---

[40] http://www.iitd.ac.in
[41] http://www.iitkgp.ac.in

#	Institute	Course	Admission
		Engineering (http://www.iitkgp.ac.in/academics)	
4	IIT Roorki[42]	B.Tech. Biotechnology (http://www.iitr.ac.in/departments/BT)	
5	IIT Madras[43]	5-year Dual Degree (M.Tech.) in Biological Engineering: (B.Tech-M.Tech)	
6		5-year Dual Degree (M.S.) in Biological Science: (B.S.-M.S.)	

❑❑❑

---

[42] http://www.iitr.ac.in
[43] https://biotech.iitm.ac.in/

103

15
Research in Science

Research in Science is a career path for those who want to systematically investigate and invent new things in science, in order to establish facts and reach conclusions.

Scientists like to discover new things, write about them and have their peers check their research. This is the basic nature of research. Scientific research is a systematic investigation of scientific theories and hypotheses. A hypothesis is a proposition of something based on available knowledge, which needs to be further explained after further experimentation. Scientists, based on their observations, formulate a hypothesis, test the hypothesis with experiments, analyse their results to see whether their hypothesis was right or wrong. People who create such hypothesis, experiments and come up with results are researchers.

Scientific researchers are involved in generating a theory to explain why something is happening and try to find answers by using various scientific experiments. This process opens up new areas for further study and continued refinement of the hypotheses. Through research scientists can test their own and others theories. Thus research is a continuous process of correcting and refining hypotheses, which might lead to certain scientific truths.

Research is to see what everybody else has seen, and to think what nobody else has thought.

-Albert Szent-Gyorgyi
(Medical Physiologist, Nobel Laureate)

Important qualities required to be a researcher are: natural inquisitiveness, analytical skills, attention to detail and most importantly "patience", and "perseverance"! This is mainly because, an experiment needs to be repeated again and again, accuracy in measuring and meticulous record keeping is required. Sometimes a research might get challenged by other researchers and might be proven wrong. Even, the geniuses like Newton, Einstein also went through such phases of struggle. But it was their patience and perseverance that made them prove their hypotheses right, making them the legends of scientific research.

Now a day, many students are opting for research in sciences, especially the natural sciences as a career. The natural sciences seek to understand how the world and universe around us works. Natural science can be broken into two main branches: life science (or biological science) and physical science. Physical science is further broken down into: physics, chemistry and Earth Sciences. All of these branches of natural science are further divided into many specialised branches or fields, and each of these is known as a "natural science". The flowchart below gives an overview of the natural sciences and some of their specialised branches or fields:

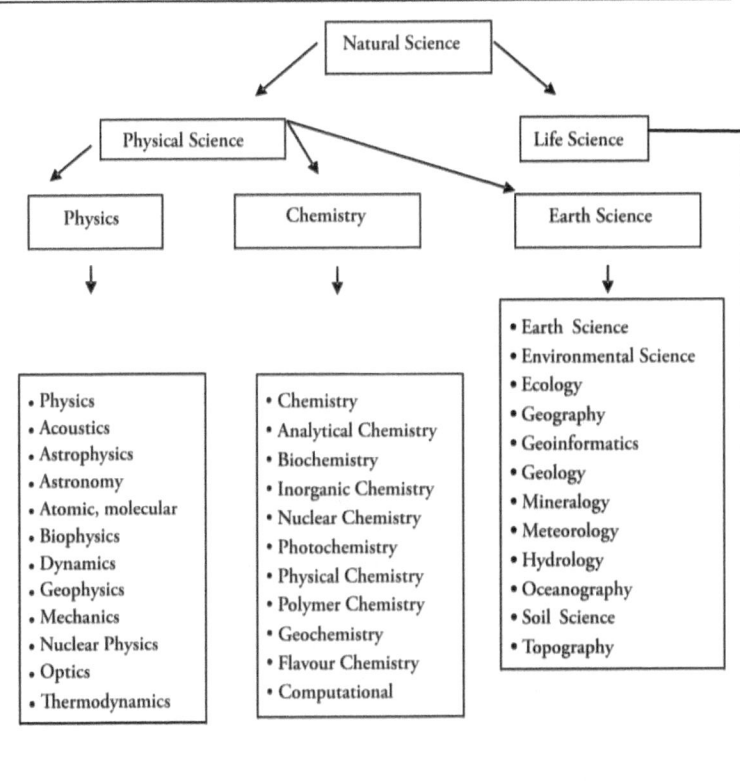

Chart 15.1

Table 15.1			
#	Institute	Course	Eligibility
1	*Indian Institute of Science Education & Research (IISER) in: Bhopal[44], Kolkata[45], Mohali[46], Pune[47], Thiruvananthapuram[48], Tirupati[49]	5-year BS-MS Dual Degree Program in Biology / Chemistry / Physics / Mathematics / Earth & Climate Science	• Through JEE Advance • Through State or Central Boards (SCB) - (10+2) with Science + IISER Aptitude Test • Through Kishore Vaigyanik Protsahan Yojana (KVPY)
2	*National Institute of Science Education & Research (NISER), Bhubaneswar, Odisha http://www.niser.ac.in/	5-year Integrated MSc programme in- Biology, Chemistry, Mathematics and Physics	• Through National Entrance Screening Test (NEST) http://www.nestexam.in/ • Eligibility : 10+2
3	*Centre for Excellence in Basic Sciences, University of Mumbai	5-year Integrated MSc programme in- Biology, Chemistry, Mathematics and Physics	• Through National Entrance Screening Test (NEST) http://www.nestexam.in/ • Eligibility : 10+2

---

[44] https://www.iiserbhopal.ac.in
[45] http://www.iiserkol.ac.in
[46] http://www.iisermohali.ac.in
[47] http://www.iiserpune.ac.in
[48] http://www.iisertvm.ac.in
[49] http://www.iisertirupati.ac.in

4	*Indian Institute of Science (IISc), Bangalore	4-year B.S.(Research) Program in Biology / Chemistry / Earth & Environmental Science / Materials / Mathematics / Physics	• JEE - Main • JEE - Advance • All India Pre Medical Test (AIPMT)
5	IIT Delhi	5- year Dual Degree: B.Tech. + M.Tech. in Biochemical Engineering & Biotechnology	• JEE Advance
		4- year B.Tech in Biochemical Engineering & Biotechnology	
6	IIT Banaras Hindu University	5- year Integrated M.Tech in Biomedical Engineering	• JEE Advance
		5- year Dual Degree: B.Tech in Bioengineering + Biomedical Technology	
7	IIT Roorki	4- year B.Tech. in Physics	• JEE Advance
8	IIT Bombay	5- year Dual Degree: B.Tech+M.Tech. in Aerospace Engineering / Physics	• JEE Advance

The general pathway towards career in scientific research: At the undergraduate level, i.e. after the 12th standard, a student opts for main subjects such as Physics, Chemistry, Biology (Botany, Zoology, Microbiology, Biotechnology) or the Earth Sciences like Geology, Geography, Environmental Science. The opportunity to research in a particular sub-field is possible at the Masters' Level and further into a niche area, at the time of Doctoral Study. The most common undergraduate course offered by all universities is the 3-year Bachelor of Science (B.Sc.) course. Admissions are given by individual colleges and the eligibility criteria are: 12th standard in science stream. Decision to conduct an entrance test or not, is left with respective college.

At the national level, excellent undergraduate or integrated graduate (5-year B.Sc. + M.Sc.) in the various streams of science are offered by prestigious institutions like IISER, NISER, IISc, IIT, BIT, etc. The details of these courses are given below:

Indian Institute of Science Education and Research (IISER): The Government of India, based on the recommendation of Scientific Advisory Council to the Prime Minister, through the Ministry of Human Resource Development (MHRD), has established the Indian Institutes of Science Education & Research (IISER). These are a group of most premier science education and research institutes in India. They have been declared by Act of Parliament as institutions of national importance, and are intended to be the IITs of basic sciences. There are currently six IISERs established across the country, and two more, one in Brahmapur and other in Nagaland has been proposed. The six IISERs are:

i. IISER Kolkata ii. IISER Pune iii. IISER Mohali	IISER Bhopal IISER Thiruvananthapuram IISER Tirupati

The main goal of the IISERs is to create quality education and research in basic sciences, and to establish advanced Research Laboratories and Central facilities for students as well as faculty.

- **The** National **Institute of Science Education and Research (NISER)**[50] is a research institute in Bhubaneswar, Odisha, operating under the Department of Atomic Energy (DAE)[51]. It offers a 5-year integrated M.Sc. and PhD in pure and applied sciences. Admissions are given through a separate entrance test namely National Entrance Screening Test (NEST)[52].

- **Centre for Excellence in Basic Sciences (CBS)**[53] is an autonomous institute affiliated to University of Mumbai, under the Department of Atomic Energy (DAE). It offers a 5-year integrated M.Sc. in science and research opportunities. Admissions are given through NEST.

- **Indian Institute of Science (IISc)**[54]: IISc is a public university for scientific research and higher education, located in Bangalore. Originally founded with the active support of Jamsetji Tata, the university now has

---

[50] http://www.niser.ac.in

[51] http://dae.nic.in

[52] https://www.nestexam.in

[53] http://www.cbs.ac.in

[54] http://www.iisc.ernet.in

a deemed university status. Along with masters and doctoral degrees, IISc also offers a four-year Bachelor of Science (Research) course in six disciplines, details of which are given in table no 15.1. The course aims at exposing the students to the inter-disciplinary nature in which scientific research is done in many upcoming fields. Admissions are given through JEE Advance or AIPMT scores.

> To raise new questions, new possibilities, to regard old problems from a new angle, requires creative imagination and marks real advance in science.
>
> -Albert Einstein

16

Microbiology

Microbiology is the study of microscopic organisms like bacteria, protozoal parasites, viruses and fungi. Those who are interested in research, there is a scope for research in two broad areas: pure and applied microbiology.

The sub-branches of pure microbiology are: Bacteriology (study of bacteria), Virology (study of viruses), Mycology (study of fungi), Parasitology (study of parasites), Immunology (study of immune system), and Phycology (study of algae). They have a considerable overlap with other disciplines of life sciences such as Biochemistry, Botany, Zoology, Cell Biology, Biotechnology etc.

The areas of applied Microbiology are:

- **Medical Microbiology**: Study of pathogenic microbes and their role in human illness
- **Pharmaceutical Microbiology**: Those related to the production of antibiotics, enzymes, vitamins, vaccines or other pharmaceutical products
- **Industrial Microbiology**: Use in industrial processes such as industrial fermentation (production of cheese, bread, wine, beer, enzymes, proteins, food supplements, etc.), waste water treatment, pollution control, etc.
- **Biotechnology**: Manipulation of micro-organisms at genetic or molecular level. This maybe regarded the

crux of biotechnology; however, the applications in this field are tremendous in scope. Production of recombinant DNA with the help of a bacteria is one such example.

- **Food Technology**: use of micro-organisms to produce food; study of micro-organisms that cause food spoilage; and food borne diseases
- **Agriculture**: Plant pathology and soil microbiology
- **Environmental**: Ecology and Geo-microbiology - associated with the environment or earth

Career opportunities in microbiology are available in research and development laboratories, hospitals and healthcare, pharmaceutical, food, agriculture, beverage, and chemical industries. Depending on their level of education microbiologists are hired as technical support staff, researchers or teachers.

Many universities offer undergraduate to doctoral level courses in Microbiology. The entry point on the career path is at the undergraduate i.e. B.Sc. Microbiology level.

17

Environmental Science

Environmental Science is a branch of Earth Sciences, a subgroup of the Natural Sciences. It is the science of the interactions between the physical, chemical, and biological components of the environment, including their effects on all types of organisms; but more often refers to the impact of human activities on the environment. Like all other natural or pure sciences, there is a great potential for research in this area hence the actual potential for career growth will be available at PhD or at least after the Master's course.

Environmental Biologists work in the following areas:

- Environmental Pollution and Control
- Conservation and Management of Natural Resources
- Ecology and Biodiversity
- Environmental awareness and education

Undergraduate course in Environmental Science:

- Indian Institute of Science (IISc), Bangalore offers a 4-year Bachelor of Science (B.Sc.) Research Course in Environmental Science which is offered by the Department of Earth and Environmental Science. It is a multidisciplinary course offering the fundamentals of Physics, Chemistry, Mathematics, and Biology as well as a basic foundation in the principles of Engineering in the initial years of the course. In the subsequent years students are taught Environmental Chemistry, Earth Science, Atmospheric Science and Environmental Engineering. Admission details for this course are given in (Table 15.1).

- Some universities also offer a **3-year Bachelor of Environmental Science Course** (B.Sc. Environmental Science). Eligibility criteria for the same 12th standard in Science Stream. Admissions are done by the individual colleges offering the course; there is no centralised admission process.

❑❑❑

18

Defence (Armed Forces)

Armed forces not only include combat forces but also include supporting forces such as doctors, nurses, engineers, accountants, logistic experts, legal experts, administrative staff etc. For joining the combat forces one must be physically and mentally fit, possess an ability to endure harsh conditions and leadership skills, have perseverance, dedication, discipline and must put the nation above anything else. Combat forces often have to spend long periods of time in diverse conditions, away from their families. For the supporting forces also the same characteristics are applicable. Although they do not have to participate in actual combat, the medical team, engineers etc. accompany the combat forces in their bases thus face similar conditions. A career in the Armed Forces holds promise of honour, glory, privileged life style and a high standing in society.

The Indian Armed Forces are the military forces of India which consist of four professional uniformed services: The Indian Army, Indian Air Force, Indian Navy, and Indian Coast Guard. The various paramilitary organisations and various inter-service institutions also help the Indian Armed Forces.

Recruitment in Indian Armed Forces:

The first level at which one may gain entry into this field, as a Commissioned Officer in the Armed Forces, is after the 12th standard; one may choose from the Indian Army, Indian Navy,

Indian Air Force, or the Armed Forces Medical College. The National Level Entrance Exam for the same is conducted by the Union Public Service Commission (UPSC: http://www.upsc.gov.in). However, one can seek entry into the Indian Coast Guards as an officer, only after completing graduation.

Aspiring students then have another chance to enter Armed Forces as a commissioned officer, after graduation. Any degree like B.E., B.Tech., B.Sc., B.Com., B.A. etc. makes you eligible to seek admission into Armed Forces.

There are two ways in which students may seek admission into the Armed Forces after completing the 12th Standard exam.

A. Entry in National Defence Academy (NDA) through UPSC examination:

National Defence Academy (NDA) is a premier joint training institution and center of excellence for grooming junior leaders for the Indian armed forces (Army, Navy and Air Force). The academy aims to train and equip the cadets with mental, moral and physical attributes required to cope with the challenges of the future battle field with the aim of leading troops to victory. The candidates are given preliminary training, both academic and physical for a period of 3 years at NDA. The training during the first two and half years is common to the cadets of all the three wings - army, navy, as well as air force. On successfully completing the course, the Army and Air Force cadets are awarded a **B.Sc. / B.Sc. (Computer) / B.A. degree from Jawaharlal Nehru University, Delhi**; while the Navy cadets have an option to major in Electronics and Communication Engineering, Mechanical

117

Engineering, or Naval Architecture, and are awarded a **Bachelor of Technology** degree. Cadets majoring in Naval Architecture have to undergo an additional 6 months of training at the Naval Dockyard, Visakhapatnam after graduation.

On passing out from the National Defence Academy, Army Cadets go to the **Indian Military Academy (IMA), Dehra Dun,** for a 1-year military training; the Naval Cadets go to **Indian Naval Academy (NA), Ezhimala,** for a 1-year training for the Executive Branch; and the Air Force cadets join **Air Force Academy (AFA), Hyderabad,** for a 1.5 year training course before they are given a permanent commission into the Armed Forces.

Admission Process for entry in NDA:

- Eligibility criteria: Age – 16.5 to 19.5 year; Sex – Male; Qualification (for Army) – successfully completed 12th standard; Qualification (for Air Force and Navy) – successfully completed 12th standard with Physics and Mathematics
- A written examination is conducted by UPSC twice a year (April and September)
- Written exam consists of two papers, Paper 1-Mathematics for 300 marks and Paper 2-General Ability Test for 600 marks. All questions are multiple-choice based questions. The syllabus is declared by UPSC every 6 months. Mathematics questions are based on Algebra, Matrices and Determinants, Trigonometry, Analytics Geometry, Vector Algebra etc. The General Ability papers consist of two parts, part 1-English (200 marks) and part 2-General

Knowledge (400 marks) which contains Physics, Chemistry, General Science, Social Science and Current Affairs.

- Tip: As you have observed, Maths is not compulsory for being eligible for Army hence candidate from any stream can appear for NDA-Army Entrance Exam. However, Mathematics is an integral part of the test; hence it is advisable to keep mathematics in 11th and 12th standards. To utilise maximum age limit and test attempts, do submit the online application at the time of end of 11th standard (April/May) or in the subsequent month of October/November.

- Usually the results of the written exam are declared in mid-July and mid-December on the UPSC website.

- Candidates who qualify in the written examination are called for the Service Selection Board (SSB) Interview.

- The **SSB** Interview lasts 5 days, and consists of two broad stages. Stage one is on Day 1 of the interview; it consists of only psychological tests: Intelligence Test, Picture Perception and Description Test (PPDT), and Personal Questionnaire Filling (PIQ). Only the candidates selected through these tests on Day 1 are requested to stay; they subsequently undergo further assessment.

- Day 2 consists of some more psychological tests like Word Association Test (WAT), Thematic Apperception Test (TAT), Situation Reaction Test (SRT), and Self-Description Test

- On Day 3 and 4, the candidates are divided into small groups and Group Testing Officer tests each group. The candidates are observed and assessed through group tasks, and the tests administered are Group

Discussion test, Military Planning Exercise (MPE), Lectures, Progressive Group Task (PGT), Intergroup Obstacle race or Snake race, Half Group Task, Command Task. Simultaneously some candidates also undergo personal interviews. The interview continues for about 45 min to 1 hour where, a candidate's potential to be a good officer, and his physical and mental fortitude are assessed.

- On Day 4, remaining assessments like Individual obstacles test and Final Group Tasks are assessed and the remaining candidates undergo their interviews.

- On the 5th Day each candidate faces the whole selection board and names of the final selected candidates are declared.

- After the SSB interview the candidates undergo Medical fitness test and the selected candidates are sent to the respective Training academy.

- Candidates who wish to join Indian Air Force have to give an additional test called Pilot Battery Aptitude Test (PABT) during the SSB interview of Air Force. This test is aimed at assessing a candidate's aptitude to be trained as a pilot. It consists of three tests: Instrument Battery Test, Sensory Motor Apparatus Test and Control Velocity Test.

B. Technical Entry after 12th standard in Army and Navy:

As mentioned previously, there are two ways in which students may seek admission into the Armed Forces after completing the 12th Standard exam, and the second method is by opting for a technical entry.

120

The Technical Entry Scheme is a viable option only for candidates who wish to join Army or Navy. This entry is for the permanent commission as a Technical Officer in Army and Navy.

Entry Process: (Table 18.1)

	Army	Navy
Notification	Twice in year - in April/May and September/October	Twice in year - in May/June and September
Sex	Male	Male
Age at the time of applying	16-19 years	16.5 - 19 years
Age at the time of joining	16.5 - 19.5 years	17 - 19.5 years
Qualification	12th Science with 70% and above in PCM	12th Science with 70% in PCM + 50% and above in English in either 10th or 12th
Apply online to	www.joinindianarmy.nic.in	www.joinindiannavy.nic.in
Selection Process	Merit + SSB Interviews	Merit + SSB Interviews
	4-years Technical Training and Bachelor of Engineering Degree (B.E.) from Jawaharlal Nehru University (JNU)	4-years B.Tech. course at Naval Academy, Ezhimala, Kerala. Degree from JNU

- There is no Technical Entry in Indian Air Force possible after 12ᵗʰ standard. The next entry point for Indian Air Force is at Graduate Level through Combined Defence Services Examination conducted by UPSC. This option is also available for entry in Indian Army and Navy. For more information please visit the UPSC[55] website.

- **Indian Coast Guard**: eligibility to seek admission as officer in the Indian Coast Guard is at Graduate level. Details are available on the website of Indian Coast Guard[56].

C. Armed Forces Medical College (AFMC):

- Admissions to the MBBS Course are done through the All India Pre-Medical Test (AIPMT) and the AFMC Aptitude Test. From now onwards, it will be NEET in place of AIPMT.

- **Eligibility criteria -**

  ✓ 12ᵗʰ standard with English, Physics, Chemistry and Biology/Biotechnology.
  ✓ Age: 17-22 years for 12ᵗʰ pass or Below 24 for B.Sc.
  ✓ Number of seats: 135 (25 for girls). This is the only course in Armed Forces for girls at the 12ᵗʰ standard level. Entry in all branches of the Armed Forces is possible for girls at the graduate level.

---

[55] http://www.upsc.gov.in/general/cds.htm
[56] http://www.joinindiancoastguard.gov.in/officerentry.html

- Those who want to apply to AFMC need to register on the AIPMT[57] website and have to select the option for AFMC while registering.
- In addition to the AIPMT registration, the student also needs to register on AFMC[58][59] websites.
- On the declaration of AIPMT results, AFMC Pune declares a merit list from the candidates who have selected AFMC option while registering.
- Qualifying marks are 50th percentile.
- The selected candidates have to appear for the Test of English Language, Comprehension, Logic and Reasoning (ToELR) and Psychological assessment cum Interview. The candidates qualifying in these are finally selected.

The following flowchart summarises the different modes of entry in the Armed Forces after 12th standard:

When you go home tell them of us and say, for your tomorrow we gave our today

...A soldier

---

[57] http://aipmt.nic.in

[58] http://www.afmc.nic.in

[59] http://www.afmcdg1d.gov.in/

Chart: 18.1

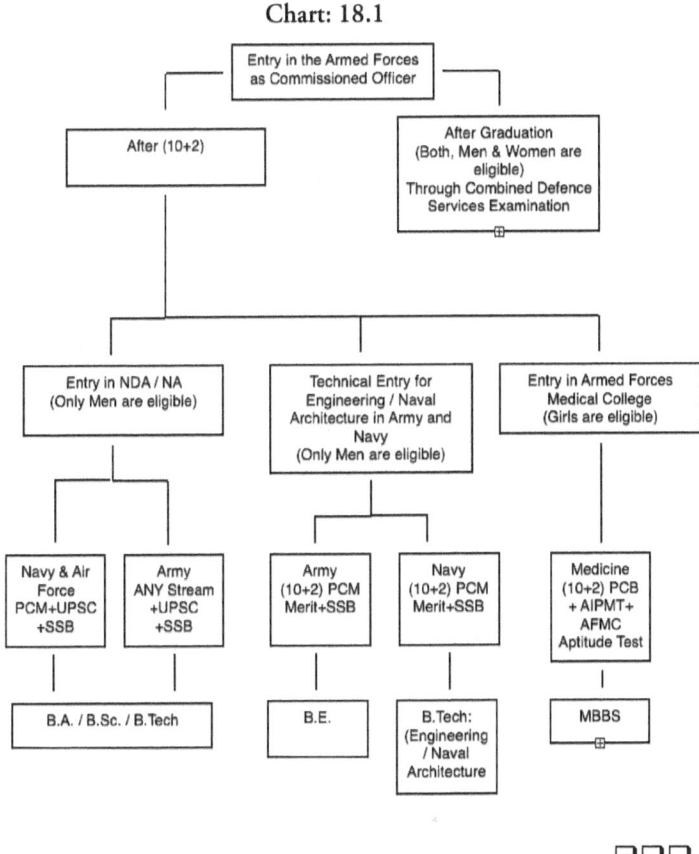

19

Chartered Accountant (CA)

Chartered accountants offer financial advice, audit accounts, create financial reports and provide information about taxation, auditing, forensic accounting, corporate finance, business recovery and insolvency, or accounting systems and processes. In other words, they monitor and document the flow of money by managing financial statements and accounts.

How to become a Chartered Accountant:

The Institute of Chartered Accountants in India (ICAI) is the statutory body established under the Chartered Accountants Act, 1949 to regulate the profession of Chartered Accountants in India. The CA examination is designed, developed, and regulated by ICAI. A person can become a member of ICAI after passing the CA Final Examination, initially as an Associate Member and then a Fellow Member after completing 5 years as a professional or 10 years in employment.

The entry level to become a Chartered Accountant is: after passing the 10th standard examination, after passing the Common Proficiency Test (CPT), or after completing B.Com.

A. Common Proficiency Test (CPT):

1. Enrol with the Institute for Common Proficiency Course (CPC) after passing class 10th standard examination.

2. Appear in CPT examination after appearing in 12th standard examination. The 12th standard examination of almost all Boards (HSC/CBSE/ICSC etc.) is usually held in February/March. The CPT exam is held twice a year - June and December. Thus one can start preparing for the examination in 11th standard itself or latest by the beginning of 12th standard. A student must register at least 60 days in advance from the date of CPT, thus students registered on or before 1st April/1st October are eligible to appear in June/December examination respectively

3. There are two papers of total 200 marks. Paper-1 contains 50-marks questions on account achy and 50-marks for Law. Paper-2 contains 50-marks for Quantitative aptitude and 50-marks for Economics

4. After passing the CPT and 12th standard examination, a student is eligible to join the **Intermediate Integrated Professional Competency Course.** This course consists of the following:

- Undergo 35-hours Orientation program.
- Complete 100-hours of ITT (Information Technology Training).
- Complete the 8-month study course before appearing for the **Intermediate (IPC) Examination.**
- Appear in Intermediate (IPC) Examination on completion of 8 months of study.

- Join articled training (Article-ship) after passing either Group 1 or both Groups (Group 1 and 2) of Intermediate (IPC) Course.
- Article-ship is a 3-year practical training phase during which the students have to work on real assignments for real employers (mostly Chartered Accountant firms).
- Undergo First General Management and Communication Skills (GMCS) course (15-days) during the first year of articled training
- Undergo Second General Management and Communication Skills (GMCS) course (15-days) after completion of 18 months of articled training but before completion of articled training. Alternatively, attend Four Week's Residential Programme on Professional Skills Development.
- Clear Group II of Intermediate (IPC) Examination if not done earlier.

5. Join CA Final Course:

- After passing Intermediate (IPC) Examination register for Final course and register for the CA Final Examination.
- Complete Advance Information Technology Training during the third year of practical training (article-ship) but before appearing in the Final Examination.

1. Appear for the CA Final Exam after completing the Article-ship or in the last 6 months of articled-ship.
2. Enrol as a member of the ICAI and be designate as "Chartered Accountant" after passing the CA Final Examination.

B. **Direct Entry:** Commerce Graduate/Post-graduates with 55% are eligible to enrol directly into the IPCC Group 1 and 2 and then follow the other steps similar to that of the CPT route

Detailed information is available on ICAI[60] website.

Note:

- Technically, students from ALL streams (11th-12th) are eligible to appear for the CPT examination and Graduates from all streams are eligible to appear for IPC examination. But the subject and work area are so closely related that only students from commerce stream prefer to do this course.

20

Company Secretary (CS)

A Company Secretary (CS) is involved in the efficient management of the corporate sector, with a primary duty to ensure compliances with various legislations like financial, labour related, industrial, and economic law related. For this purpose, a CS has to interact, coordinate, integrate, and cooperate with various other functional heads in a company. He acts as a confidante of the board of directors and counsels the Board of Directors and other functional heads on the legal implications of any proposal under consideration. Hence the Company Secretary needs to have a multidisciplinary background in law, management and finance. The job of a Company Secretary also involves diverse responsibilities such as formulating long-term and short-term corporate policies and programmes, accounting and finance functions, tax planning and management etc.

Career Prospects:

- As per the Companies Act, companies having a paid-up capital of Rs.5 crores or more, have to appoint a full-time Company Secretary. Paid-up capital is the amount of money investors have invested into the company since it's inception by buying the equity shares of the company.

- In an employment, company secretaries may hold important positions in the secretarial, legal, finance, accounts, personnel and administrative functions in the private as well as public sector.

- It is also one of the essential qualifications for recruitment to Grades I to IV in the Accounts Branch of the Central Company Law Service of the Central Government.
- Almost every kind of organisation whose affairs are controlled by boards, councils and other corporate structures be it a co-operative, trust, society, association, federation, statutory authority, commission, board or the like, finds it useful to appoint a Company Secretary in key administrative positions.
- Professional Institutes and educational bodies also consider utilisation of the services of Company Secretaries on full or part-time basis for academic or research assignments in the fields of accountancy, law or management. Besides, Department of Personnel and Administrative Reforms of the Central Government empanels Company Secretaries as professionals for assignment
- A Company Secretary can also practice independently as a professional
- Persons holding the CS qualification are eligible for admission to a PhD (Doctorate) degree. Or if they want to pursue the Cost Accountancy Course, they are exempt from the Foundation Examination of Cost Accountancy.

The Institute of Company Secretaries of India (http://www.icsi.edu) is the professional body in India, responsible to develop and regulate the profession of Company Secretaries in India. It conducts the company secretary course and examination.

The Company Secretary Course:

The Institute of Company Secretaries of India (ICSI) imparts training in Company Secretary-ship via distance education. Course material is provided to the students at the time of registration. A provision for optional oral coaching is also available.

Stages to become a company secretary:

There are two levels where a student can join the the Company Secretary course: (A) after 12th standard and (B) after graduation

A) After 12th standard:

- There are three stages of the course for students who want to pursue the course after 12th standard. They are:

  - **Foundation Program**
  - **Executive Program**
  - **Professional Program**
  - **Foundation Program:**

- Eligibility: 12th standard from a recognised board. There is NO minimum requirement of marks in 12th standard to appear for the examination. The student has to provide a proof of passing the 12th standard examination within 6 months of registering for the exam.

- Examination is conducted twice a year – June and December.

- Last date of applying to the December examination is 31st March of the same year. And the last date of applying for the June examination is 30th September of the previous year.

- A student can appear for the examination after completion of minimum period of 8 months from the date of admission (excluding the month of admission and examination)

- The examination is for 400 marks and conducted in 4 parts:
  o Part 1: Business Environment and Entrepreneurship: 100 marks
  o Part 2: Business Management, Ethics and Communication: 100 marks
  o Part 3: Business Economics: 100 marks
  o Fundamentals of Accounting and Auditing: 100 marks

- Results of the Foundation exam are usually declared after two months

- Students, passing the Foundation Program are eligible to enrol for the Executive program

- **Executive Program: (12th standard/Graduate Mode)**

- Eligibility for Executive Program:

  a. Either Pass the Foundation Program OR
  b. Eligible for exemption (Exemption is granted to a person who is a graduate or holds a Master's degree

in ANY discipline other than Fine Arts/Passed the Foundation Examination of the Institute of Cost Accountants (CMA)/Passed the Common Proficiency Test (CPT) conducted by the Institute of Chartered Accountants (ICAI). *A non-commerce graduate needs to self-study four subjects from the Foundation Course

- There are two modules - Module 1 and Module 2 of the Executive Program. Module 1 has 4 subjects while Module 2 has 3 subjects

  i. Module1: Company Law, Cost and Management Accounting, Economic and Commercial Laws, Tax Laws and Practice
  ii. Module 2: Company Accounts and Auditing Practices, Capital Markets and Securities Laws, Industrial, Labour and General Laws

- A candidate will be admitted to the Executive Programme examination, if —

  (i) The student has registered at least nine months prior to December (when examination for both modules is conducted), which means that the student needs to register for the December examination in February of the same year or earlier and is eligible to appear for both modules. Students registering between March and August are eligible to appear for examination of both modules to be held in June of the next calendar year.

(ii) The student is eligible to appear for the examination ONLY after completing the compulsory coaching and computer training.

(iii) Those students who are registered at least six calendar months prior to the month in which exam is conducted, are eligible to appear for only one module at a time. So a student registering in March, April and May can appear for any one module in December examination and those registering in September, October and November can appear to any one group in the June examination of the next year.

(iv) The student has to undergo a course of postal or oral tuition for the module(s) to which s/he intends to appear in the examination

(v) The student has to successfully complete the Student Induction Program (SIP) and computer training program specified by the Council

- **Compulsory Management Training:** The student has to undergo compulsory management training for 15 months in companies sponsored by ICSI or under the guidance of a Company Secretary in Practice or a Firm of Company Secretaries in Practice, after passing the Executive Program

- **Professional Program:**

- There are three modules in the Professional Program.

- Eligibility for admission and Examination of Professional Program: A candidate will be admitted to the Professional Programme examination, if —

(i) The student has registered at least nine calendar months prior to the month in which the examination is held. Students registering in February or before are eligible to appear for the examination of all three modules held in December of that year while those registering between March and August are eligible to appear for all three modules in the Examination held in June of next calendar year subject to satisfactory completion compulsory coaching.

(ii) However, a candidate registering at least six calendar months prior to the month in which the examination is held, can appear in any one or two module(s) of the Professional Programme examination. For e.g. a candidate registering in March, April and May in a year will be eligible for appearing in one or two module(s) in December examination and those who are registering in September, October and November can appear in any one or two module(s) to be held in the month of June next year

(iii) The student should undergo the postal or oral tuition for the module(s)

Detailed information can be found on the ICSI[61] website.

---

[61] http://www.icsi.edu

21

Cost and Management Accountant (CMA)

A Cost and Management Accountant (CMA) is a person who is involved in services like costing, pricing of goods, and services. The cost accountant closely analyse the costs, devise ways to reduce costs. They assist in planning, monitoring and controlling the cost and price of a product or a service. They are also expected to evaluate the operating efficiency and effectiveness of production and service management by collecting, compiling, organising, verifying, comparing and analysing information from different departments of the organisation. The process involves critical monitoring of relevant costs like material, labour, overhead and capital costs etc., involved in making a product or providing a service. They analyse the sales trend to strike a balance between the demand and supply, to prevent over production. They also monitor the performance, to spot and report on problems and prevent them from occurring in future. This analysis helps in comparing the financial performances, making assessments and projections, providing figures for future costing and pricing policies and other managerial decisions. Their roles can be as below:

- Corporate Decision Making
- Resource Management
- Performance Management
- Financial Reporting and Strategy
- Optimisation of Stakeholder's value

- Risk Management
- Enterprise Governance
- Audit assurance and Taxation
- Sustainable Development
- Corporate Social Responsibility

The candidates who intend to pursue CMA course should qualify in the three stages of the course:

i.   Foundation Course
ii. Intermediate Course
iii. Final Course

i.   Foundation Course:

- **Eligibility:** 12ᵗʰ standard ANY stream, from a recognised board and should be minimum 17 years old. Duration of the course is for 8 months.

- One can join CMA Foundation Course and is offered provisional admission to the Course while pursuing 11ᵗʰ and 12ᵗʰ standard. However, the student shall be eligible to appear Foundation Course Examination only after passing 12ᵗʰ standard Examination. So, qualifying 12ᵗʰ standard examination makes the student eligible to get converted from Provisional to Regular status.

- The examination is held four times in a year and the candidate has to register atlas 4 months prior to the exam date. The following table shows the months the exam is held and the last dates of registration for each examination:

For June Examination of the same calendar year	31ˢᵗ January
For September Examination of the same calendar year	30ᵗʰ April
For December Examination of the same year	31ˢᵗ July
For March Examination of the next calendar year	31ˢᵗ October

- There are four papers of 100 marks each - Fundamentals of Economics and Management, Fundamentals of Accounting, Fundamentals of Laws and Ethics, Fundamentals of Business Mathematics and Statistics

ii. **Intermediate Course:**

- **Eligibility:** Graduate from any stream. Although, graduate from any stream is eligible, Commerce graduates find it much easier because the subjects are commerce related.
- A candidate can join CMA Intermediate Course while pursuing graduation but will be eligible to appear Intermediate Course only after qualifying Graduation Examination.
- The entrance examination is held twice in a year - June and December. To be eligible for the June examination, students have to register before 31ˢᵗ January of the same calendar year and for the December examination before 31ˢᵗ July of the same calendar year.

- Duration of the course is 18 months. It consists of group discussions, Business Communication and 100-hour Computer Training.
- There are 8 papers in this examination. The exam is conducted in two stages. The subjects are:

1) Financial Accounting
2) Laws, Ethics and Governance
3) Direct Taxation
4) Cost accounting and financial management
5) Operation Management Information System
6) Cost and Management Accounting
7) Indirect Taxation
8) Company Accounts and Audit

iii.   Final Course:

- **Eligibility**: Should pass all 8 subject-exams of the Intermediate Course.
- Course duration of 18 months and contains Dissertation and 9-Day Modular Training.
- There are 8 papers and the exam is conducted in two stages.

1) Corporate Laws and Compliance
2) Advanced Financial Management
3) Business Strategy and Strategic Cost Management
4) Tax Management and Practice
5) Strategic Performance Management
6) Corporate Financial Reporting
7) Cost and Management Audit
8) Financial Analysis and Business Valuation

Skills required for a Cost Accountant:

Cost accountants should have good negotiation skills to confirm a deal, within the available budget. They should possess good computer skills for using different accounting software. Communication skill is the most important quality needed for a cost accountant. They should have the skill to make strategic decisions and independent judgments in crucial situations. Detailed information is available on the ICMAI[62] website.

Many of the students choosing Commerce Stream wish to pursue either Chartered Accountancy, or Company Secretary, or Cost Accountancy as their career paths. The table below gives a snapshot of these three careers:

Table 21.1

	CA	CS	CMA
What should they know?	Knowledge of every aspect of accounting, audition and taxation	Knowledge of corporate law, corporate governance, ethics, corporate social responsibility, risk management	Knowledge of cost and financial management to ensure a balance between expenditures and available resources

[62] http://icmai.in

	CA	CS	CMA
What do they do?	offer financial advice, audit accounts and provide information about financial records through financial reporting, taxation, auditing, forensic accounting, corporate finance, business recovery and insolvency, or accounting systems and processes.	responsible for the efficient administration of a company, with regard to ensuring compliance with statutory and regulatory requirements and implementation of decisions of the board of directors	task of collecting, analysing, summarising and evaluating various alternative courses of action
Statutory Body	Institute of Chartered Accountants of India	Institute of Company Secretaries of India	Institute of Cost Accountants of India

Accounting does not make corporate earnings or balance sheets more volatile. Accounting just increases the transparency of volatility in earnings.

-Diane Garnick (American Investment Strategist)

141

22
Bachelor of Business Administration (BBA)

The Bachelor of Business Administration (B.B.A.) is a bachelor's degree in commerce and business administration. The degree is conferred after three years of full-time study in one or more areas of business specialisations. The B.B.A. program usually includes general business courses and advanced courses for specific concentrations.

The degree is designed to give a broad knowledge of the functional aspects of a company. The B.B.A. program exposes students to a variety of business related core subjects and allows students to specialise in a specific academic area. The degree also develops the student's practical, managerial skills, communication skills and business decision-making capability. The B.B.A. program offered by most colleges incorporates training and practical experience, in the form of case projects, presentations, internships, industrial visits, and interaction with experts from the industry.

Objectives of the B.B.A. program:

i.   To provide adequate basic understanding about management education.
ii. To prepare students to explore opportunities being newly created in the management profession.
iii. To train the students in communication skills effectively.

iv. To develop appropriate skills in the students so as to make them competent and provide themselves self-employment.

v. To inculcate entrepreneurial skills.

Eligibility:

- 12th standard from ANY stream with English, and with minimum 45% marks.

- Two years Diploma in Pharmacy after 12th standard, from an institute approved by the Board of Technical Education conducted by Government of Maharashtra or its equivalent. If a Pharmacy diploma student wants to learn business skills such as marketing, sales, accounts etc., s/he can enhance these skills by doing BBA and also will earn a degree.

- Three Year Diploma Course of Board of Technical Education conducted by Government of Maharashtra or its equivalent.

- Minimum Competency Vocational Certificate (MCVC)

- Every eligible candidate has to pass a Common Entrance Test, which is conducted by the respective Institute/College. Thus a student needs to apply to the selected colleges independently and appear for the entrance test if any.

The B.B.A. curriculum includes the following subjects:

Business Organisation and System, Communication Skills, Personality Development	E-Commerce, IT, Supply Chain Logistics

Business Laws, Taxation, Environment	Industrial Relations and Labour Laws
Business Accounting, Economics, Mathematics	Human Resource and Event Management
Principles of Marketing, Management and Finance	Entrepreneurship Development, Business Ethics

In the third year, one can choose a specialisation from 1) Finance 2) Marketing 3) Human Resource Management 4) Service Sector Management 5) Agricultural Business Management.

Career Avenues:

- Entry-level positions in many corporations and factories.
- Sales and marketing department of companies as members of sales teams or as management trainees.
- Retail management

B.B.A. is an undergraduate degree; hence a student only learns the basic management skills after completing this course. A Masters of Business Administration (M.B.A.) pursued after a B.B.A. would open more options for career development.

M.B.A.: The Master of Business Administration is a master's degree in business management (administration). This is a professional, postgraduate degree, which focuses on various areas of business such as accounting, finance, marketing, human resources and operations in a manner most relevant to management analysis and strategy. Along with the core subjects, the MBA student specializes in one subject, for e.g. Marketing, Finance, Human Resource, International Business,

Production & Materials, Computer Management etc. Eligibility to the MBA course is through and entrance exam and graduates and postgraduates from ANY stream are eligible for the entrance test.

❑❑❑

23

Law

In India, a student can pursue a legal course only after completing an undergraduate course in any discipline. However, this structure has been modified with introduction of a 5-year integrated Law degree course after passing 12th standard. In the integrated law degree course, a student gets a bachelors degree after 3 years and then continues with the legal studies for two more years to gain a Bachelor of Law (L.L.B.) degree. The Bar Council of India[63] is a supreme regulatory body that regulates the law profession. It also prescribes the minimum curriculum of the law course, recognizes the degrees, and also evaluates the teaching institutions.

Following are some areas where the lawyers can work:

- They can work as legal counsel and legal advisors for corporate sector, firms, organizations, legal persons, individuals and families.
- They can work as trustees of various trusts, as teachers, law reporters, company secretaries and so on.
- Lawyers can work in private as well as public sector and can also choose whether they want an employment or would prefer to be a independent professional.

---

[63] http://barcouncilofindia.org

A law graduate can specialise in any of the specific areas mentioned below, depending on his/her interests and inclinations. A number of courses are now available in fields like human rights, intellectual property rights, and cyber law, etc.

- **Civil Law:** Deals with the concerns of private rights of individuals, handling damage suits, breach of contract suits, drawing deeds, wills, mortgages, acting as trustee or guardian, etc.
- **Tax Law:** Deals with income tax, estate tax, real tax, franchises, inheritance, etc.
- **Criminal Law:** Deals with offences against society or state. It involves interviewing clients and interrogating witnesses, correlating findings, conducting trials, preparing a case for defence, examining, cross examining in court and so on.
- **Corporate Law:** Deals with advising companies on their legal rights, obligations, privileges; studying statutes, constitutions and ordinances; and, helping corporates to make the all-important decision of whether to go in for a suit at all.
- **International Law:** Specialises on treaties, customs and traditions observed by nations in their relations with one another.
- **Labour Law:** Deals with workers, their associations, working conditions, workers' rights and duties, etc.
- **Real Estate Law:** Covers conveyance of property, search records and deeds to establish titles of property; acting as trustee for property; and, drawing up legal documents for deeds and mortgages.

- **Patent Law/Intellectual Property Rights**: Focuses on securing patents for inventors from the patent's office. Here the lawyer specialises in prosecuting or defending patent infringement and preparing detailed specifications of the patent and so on.

- **Cyber Law**: Deals with the prevention and reduction of large scale damage from cybercriminal activities by protecting information access, privacy, communications, intellectual property (IP) and freedom of speech related to the use of the Internet, websites, email, computers, cell phones, software and hardware, such as data storage devices.

A Law graduate, after completing the mandatory article-ship, can become either an advocate or a solicitor. An advocate pleads in court and is actively involved in litigation; whereas, a solicitor offers legal advice to clients on a wide range of subjects, from personal to business matters. If a case goes to court, the solicitor briefs and advises the advocate who takes up the case on behalf of the client.

Education:

Almost all universities in India offer a degree in Law. The L.L.B. degree is awarded at the undergraduate level and LLM is awarded at the post-graduate level. There are two levels of entry for the LLB course -

i. **After 12th standard**: there is a 5-year integrated BA-LLB course. Eligibility: 12th standard from ANY stream.

    Some deemed universities also offer a 5-year integrated BBA-LLB course.

ii. **After Graduation**: This is a 3-year course. Eligibility: Graduate from ANY stream.

Admission Process:

National Law Universities: The L.L.B. and L.L.M. courses offered by the 17 National Law Universities are considered to be the Premium Courses in India. Admissions are given through the Common Law Admission Test (CLAT) which is conducted in rotation by theses 17 Universities and is generally held in April/May.

Eligibility Criteria for CLAT: 12th standard pass or appearing from ANY stream, with 45% marks. The exam is of 200 marks, with 200 questions. The exam subjects are: English including comprehension, General Knowledge and current affairs, Elementary Mathematics (Numerical Ability), Legal Aptitude and Logical Reasoning.

Admissions are given through centralised counselling through merit-cum-preference.

National Universities:

1. National Law School of India University, Bangalore (NLSIU)
2. National Academy of Legal Study and Research University of Law, Hyderabad (NALSAR)
3. The National Law Institute University, Bhopal (NLIU)
4. The West Bengal National University of Juridical Sciences, Kolkata (WBNUJS)
5. National Law University, Jodhpur (NLUJ)
6. Hidayatullah National Law University, Raipur (HNLU)

7. Gujarat National Law University, Gandhinagar (GNLU)

8. Dr. Ram Manohar Lohiya National Law University, Lucknow (RMLNLU)

9. Rajiv Gandhi National University of Law, Punjab (RGNUL)

10. Chanakya National Law University, Patna(CNLU)

11. The National University of Advanced Legal Studies, Kochi (NUALS)

12. National Law University Odisha, Cuttack (NLUO)

13. National University of Studying Researching Law, Ranchi (NUSRL)

14. National Law University and Judicial Academy, Assam (NLUJAA)

15. Damodaram Sanjivayya National Law University, Visakhapatnam (DSNLU)

16. Tamil Nadu National Law School, Tiruchirappalli (TNNLS)

17. Maharashtra National Law University, Mumbai (MNLU)

Other Government, Private Law Colleges in Maharashtra:

Earlier the colleges in Maharashtra (other than the NLUs) used to admit students independently through their own merit list. Thus the students had to apply separately to each college; this proved to be very time consuming and expensive as students had to pay the application fees to independent colleges. Understanding this, the Government of Maharashtra will be conducting a Common Entrance Test for all the Government and Private colleges in Maharashtra from the academic year 2016-17 onwards. The exam will be conducted for admissions to the 3-year L.L.B. and 5-year Integrated BA-LLB course. Details of this examination are awaited.

> We lawyers are always curious, always inquisitive, always picking up odds and ends for our patchwork minds, since there is no knowing when and where they may fit into some corner.
>
> -Charles Dickens

24

Hospitality: Hotel Management and Travel and Tourism

India is emerging as a favourite destination for tourists both for business as well as for leisure, giving a lot of scope to the service sector. This has given an impetus for growth to the **Hospitality Industry**. Hospitality can be defined as *the cordial and generous reception and entertainment of 'guests', either socially or commercially.* Hospitality Industry is a broad area comprising of hotel and tourism, which have a common goal - "Customer Satisfaction!" The primary sectors in the Hospitality Industry are:

- Accommodation (Hotels - small/big/national/multinational)
- Food Service (Restaurants and Bar/Fast Food Joints/Coffee shops/Home Deliveries etc.)
- Recreation Centres (clubs/theme parks/resorts etc.)
- Travel and Tourism (Planning/bookings, Airlines/cruise lines/various forms of travel)
- Special event planning for social (weddings) and business (exhibitions/corporate meets/conferences etc.) purpose

All these areas are primarily focused on understanding the requirements of customers and providing the appropriate services. Many students and parents get confused between Hospitality Management and Hotel Management. Hospitality

Management, as can be seen above, is a much broader term; Hotel Management is a part of   Hospitality it. Thus a student needs to be very clear which path S/he wants to pursue before selecting a course and preparing for an entrance test. The chart below gives an overview of the Hospitality Industry:

❑❑❑

24.1

Hotel Management

Hotel Management is an area of study that covers a wide range of topics concerned with the operational aspects of a hotel such as culinary, front office management, housekeeping, marketing, accounts etc. Many universities or institutes in India offer courses in hotel management at different levels such as diplomas, bachelor's degrees or masters degrees.

To introduce standard education in this sector the Government of India has established a society called **National Council for Hotel Management and Catering Technology (NCHMCT)**[64] under the ministry of Agriculture (Department of Food). The Council regulates academics activities in the field of Hospitality Education and Training that is imparted through 21 Central Government sponsored Institutes of Hotel Management, 21 State Government sponsored institutes, 15 Private institutes and 7 Food Craft Institutes, that function in different parts of the country.

Through the Council, these institutes offer 10 different professional programs leading to award of Certificate, Diploma, Post Graduate Diploma, Bachelor and Master Degree. The B.Sc. and M.Sc. programmes are offered in

---

[64] http://www.nchm.nic.in

collaboration with Indira Gandhi National Open University – IGNOU[65].

List of Bachelors, Diploma and Certificate courses:

Table 24.1

#	Course Name	Duration	Eligibility and Admission
1	B.Sc. in Hospitality and Hotel Administration - Generic	3-year	(12th standard) with English as one of the subjects + JEE Main
2	B.Sc. in Hospitality and Hotel Administration - Specialisation (Food Production/Food and Beverage/Accommodation) in 4/5/6 Semester	3-year	
3	Diploma in Food Production: 1000 seats	1-year + 24 month internship	(12th standard) with English as one of the subjects - Direct application to individual institute
4	Diploma in Food and Beverage Service: 660 seats		
5	Diploma in Bakery and Confectionary :180 seats		
6	Diploma in Front Office Operation: 230 seats		
7	Diploma in Housekeeping: 240 seats		
8	Craftsmanship Certificate Course in		10th standard with English as

#	Course Name	Duration	Eligibility and Admission
	Food Production and Patisserie : 619 seats	1-year + 20 month internship	compulsory subject - Direct application to individual institutes
9	Craftsmanship Certificate Course in Food and Beverage Service : 240 seats		

There are in all 7667 seats available for the B.Sc. in Hospitality and Hotel Administration - Generic course. Out of these, 4787 seats are available in the Central Institutes of Hotel Management (IHM), 1640 in State IHMs and 1240 in Private IHMs, all over India. Specialisation degree is coordinated at 7 institutes located at Chennai, Goa, Hyderabad, Kolkata and Mumbai. Limited seats are available and are offered based on the performance in the 1st and 2nd semester examination, based on merit-cum-choice basis. Details are available on NCHMCT website.

Bachelors Course from Birla Institute of Technology (BITS) at Mesra, Ranchi: BITS Mesra offers a 4-year B.Sc.in Hotel Management and Catering Technology (BHMCT)[66] course.

Eligibility for Entrance: 12ᵗʰ standard with English as one of the subjects with minimum 45% marks. Selection is made on the basis of performance in the Entrance Test. The test is of 100 marks – 25 marks each for English, Numerical and Data Analysis, Reasoning and Intelligence, and General Knowledge.

---

[66] https://www.bitmesra.ac.in

Common Entrance Test conducted by Government of Maharashtra:

The Directorate of Technical Education, Maharashtra State conducts a Common Entrance Test (MAH-HM-CET) to the State Government approved 4-year bachelor's degree course in Hotel Management and Catering Technology (HMCT) in the government-aided, un-aided institutes, which are AICTE approved.

Eligibility: 12ᵗʰ standard from any recognised board, with English as one of the subjects + minimum 45% marks in 12ᵗʰ standards qualifying examination. The entrance examination is of 100 marks, to be completed in 90 minutes. The syllabus consists of subjects like: Reasoning, English, and General Knowledge. More information can be found on the DTE[67] website.

The general syllabus of the bachelor's course in Hotel Management not only equips students with all required knowledge and skills in the supervisory responsibilities of the Hospitality sector, it also helps students gain appropriate skills and knowledge in the operational areas of food production, food and beverage service, front office operations, and house-keeping. It also provides managerial skills in subjects like hotel accountancy, food quality and safety, human resource management, financial management, tourism marketing, tourism management etc.

---

[67] http://dtemaharashtra.gov.in

Career opportunities for the graduates in Hospitality and Hotel management are:

- Management Trainee in Hotel and allied hospitality industry;
- Kitchen Management/Housekeeping Management positions in Hotels after initial stint as trainee;
- Flight Kitchens and on-board flight services;
- Indian Navy Hospitality services;
- Guest/Customer Relation Executive in Hotel and other Service Sectors;
- Management Trainee/Executive in international and national fast food chains;
- Hospital and Institutional Catering;
- Faculty in Hotel Management/Food Craft Institutes;
- Shipping and Cruise lines;
- Marketing/Sales Executive in Hotel and other Service Sectors;
- State Tourism Development Corporations;
- Resort Management;
- Self-employment through entrepreneurship and
- Multinational companies for their hospitality services.

Due to the tremendous growth potential in the Hospitality Industry, about 80% of the graduates are successfully employed by Hospitality and other service sectors through on-campus and off-campus recruitment processes.

24.2

Travel and Tourism

The other sector of the Hospitality Industry, which has a substantial potential for growth, is Travel and Tourism. The tourism industry is dominated by the youth, and small and medium enterprises also play an important role in it. This industry demands young people with pleasing personality and good communication skills. Some areas in the Tourism industry where one can develop his/career are:

- **Tour Operations**: This includes product and package design, itinerary preparation, file handling, marketing, ticketing and linkage with other service providers associated with the tourism trade. A person is required to have good destination knowledge and networking with suppliers.

- **Travel agencies**: They are the link between tour operators and tourists. Persons working in this area need to have IT exposure in addition to the other required skills.

- **Hotels**: Hotels and resort appoint people having exposure to tourism. All star hotels have travel desks that are handled by tourism professionals.

- **Transport/Logistics/Cargo**: All types of transports - air, road, cruise or Luxury trains where tourism professionals can work. They can also work with airlines as the ground handling staff. IRCTC also requires tourism professionals. Similarly, the cargo companies like DHL, Fedex, GATI etc also require tourism professionals for logistic handling.

- Wildlife, agri-tourism, rural tourism, safaris, bird watching etc.

Additionally, there are other ways through which one can enter the Tourism Industry. They are:

- Travel agent
- Tour operator/Guide
- Aviation - Air Hostess/Hosts, Counter/Reservation Staff, Marketing
- Cruise Ships
- Marketing Personnel
- Human Resource and many more

Training:

Indian Institute of Tourism and Travel Management (IITTM)[68] is an organisation under Ministry of Tourism, Govt. of India. It offers MBA in Tourism, which has more than 600 seats all over India. The training institutes are located in Gwalior, Bhubaneswar, Noida, Nellore and Goa. In addition to the Masters course, IITTM also conducts short certificate courses in various subjects.

IITTM also has proposed **Bachelors Course in Tourism** from the academic year 2016, for which approval is awaited. This will be a 3-year course, for which, proposed eligibility will be 12th standard with 50% marks in ANY discipline. IITTM

---

[68] www.iittm.net

will also conduct an IITTM Admission Test (IAT) in the month of May.

Various other courses are also available in Travel and Tourism Management, ranging from Certificate, Diploma, Post-Graduate Diploma, Bachelors and Masters.

Bachelor of Art in Tourism Studies (BTS): Indira Gandhi National Open University (IGNOU) offers this course. It is a 3-year Distance Education course. Eligibility: 12th standard from any stream.

Bachelor of Vocation (B. Voc.) in Tourism: This is a 3-year Bachelors course offered by Mumbai University launched under the skills development scheme of Government of India. (More details are given in the Chapter on B. Voc. Courses). Eligibility: 12th standard from ANY stream from an authorised board in India. Some of the colleges offering this course are: St. Xavier's College, H. R. College, Ramnarain Ruia College, Nagindas Khandwala College, Mumbai.

Diploma Courses: 1-year full-time or 2-year part-time Post Graduate Diploma Courses are also available in many institutes.

Certificate: The Maharashtra State Board offers a Minimum Competency Vocational Certificate (MCVC) after 10th standard. Students completing this certificate course receive the Higher Secondary Certificate and are eligible to pursue a Bachelor of Art Degree afterwards.

Aviation: Those interested in the Aviation industry can do Diploma in International/Domestic Ticketing, Diploma in Air

Hostess/Host, Flight Steward, etc. These courses are of short duration and offered by private agencies.

Cruise: This is an upcoming area, which has started receiving lot of attention due to the mushrooming of different leisure and commercial cruises. A person who's got a qualification in Hospitality, especially the Hotel management personnel have many job opportunities available in this area.

Who can choose a career in Hospitality?

Those who are ready for any amount of hard work, like to interact with different people, have good communication skills, right attitudes, patience, discipline, can do well in the hospitality industry.

Those who know at least one foreign language, have good command on English, appropriate manners and lot of patience, also have a good scope in the Tourism Industry as Tourist guides and tour operators.

> The world is a book and those who do not travel, read only one page.
>
> -St. Augustine

□□□

162

25
Arts and Humanities and Social Sciences

Arts and humanities are considered as two of the oldest fields of knowledge available to man. They include the disciplines of ancient and modern languages, literature, philosophy, visual and performing arts. These disciplines explore, share, and recreate expressions of the human experience.

"**Arts**" is anything that people create: paintings, music, dance, literature, sculpture etc.

Humanities and Social Sciences are academic disciplines that study human culture. They deal with human aspects like politics, law, linguistics, economics, and psychology. One of the major differences between the two is that humanities involve a more critical and analytical approach, whereas social sciences deal with more of a scientific approach.

Humanities are a branch of science that deals with heritage, and the question of what makes us human. Humanities deal with law, history, ancient languages, modern languages, philosophy, history and religion. Humanities are considered to be more philosophical than Social Sciences.

Social Sciences are concerned with society and the relationships among individuals with society. As there is a scientific approach to Social Sciences, it is considered to be a branch of study in between humanities and natural sciences.

Anthropology, Criminology, Administration, Archaeology, Education, Economics, Psychology, Linguistics, Political Science, Law, and History come under the purview of Social Sciences.

Humanities	Social Science
More critical and analytical approach	More scientific approach
Deal with heritage and the question of what makes us human	Deals with the study between humanities and natural sciences

Many Universities in India offer a **Bachelor of Arts (B.A.)** degree for the Arts and Humanities subjects as the undergraduate degree. The undergraduate degree in Fine Arts is now called Bachelor of Fine Arts (B.F.A.), and for subjects like Anthropology, Economics, Archaeology, some universities award a "Bachelor of Science (B.Sc.)" degree, as they fall under the Social Sciences stream.

- **Savitribai Phule Pune University**[69] (formerly Pune University) has two different faculties offering certificate, diploma, undergraduate degree and postgraduate degree programs –
- (i) Faculty of Arts and Performing Arts (Ancient and Modern Languages, Fine Arts and Performing Arts)
- (ii) Faculty of Mental and Moral Sciences (History, Archaeology, Geography, Anthropology, Mathematics, Statistics, Philosophy, Logic, Economics, Psychology, Sociology, Political Science,

---

[69] http://www.unipune.ac.in

Defence Strategies, Communication and Journalism, Library Science).

- **Mumbai University**[70] has different departments offering certificate, diploma, under-graduate and postgraduate degree programs under the Faculty of Arts. These departments are: Fine Arts, Communication and Journalism, Education, Library Science, Language-Linguistics-Literature, Social Science, and Management Studies.

- **Jawaharlal National University**[71], New Delhi has faculties such as Arts and Aesthetics, Social Sciences, Language-Literature-Cultural Studies

Admission Process for Bachelor of Arts:

- Eligibility for the Bachelor of Arts Courses in Languages, Literature, Social Sciences are decided by the individual colleges. Minimum eligibility for all these courses is 12th standard and as per the norms of each university. Usually the individual colleges give the First Year B.A. admissions, hence a students has to apply to the choses colleges independently and are admitted on the basis of merit list. Entrance tests (if any) are conducted by the colleges independently.

Some more tips for those interested in Humanities and Social Sciences:

- The Bachelor of Arts degree focuses on understanding different aspects of a society and gives an overview of

---

[70] http://mu.ac.in
[71] http://www.jnu.ac.in

various topics. In addition to the disciplinary study, it can equip one with analytical and critical thinking abilities because many subjects are interconnected.

- One should have a great interest in the subjects before opting for the Arts and Humanities stream. It is generally seen that students who are really interested in the subjects under humanities and those who have a specific goal only opt for this stream. For example a student who wants to pursue a career in Defence Strategies will choose subjects like Political Science, Sociology, Economics, etc. at the undergraduate level before opting for the Masters course in Defence Strategies.

- The bachelor course in arts and social sciences (except fine and performing arts) equips a student with knowledge and basic applied skills of the major they are graduating in and general awareness, basic knowledge about the minor subject they study in the first and second year of graduation.

- Thus while choosing a major, a student must consider and choose subjects which are supplementary to the chosen major. For example, if a student wants to pursue a major in Psychology, then Sociology is a good supplementary subject with it. If Political Science is a major, then Economics or Sociology can be the minor subjects.

- It will be a good idea to pursue parallel courses that will help in building skills (similar to those who pursue commerce graduation) while pursuing the undergraduate course. If a student is pursuing a degree in one foreign language then supplementing it with

166

another language or a computer course would be a good idea.

Career Avenues:

- Social Sciences have a distinct socio-economic, cultural and political relevance. Because of this, graduates and post-graduates are getting jobs in the public and private sector, in human resource, personnel, public relations department, training centres and RTI offices. Graduates from psychology departments are employed as counsellors by the corporate sector. As per the new Company Act, 2013, each private and public sector company has to spend 2% of its profit for corporate social responsibility (CSR) initiatives. This has opened up new avenues for students of social science and humanities for employment as project managers/ programme officers of the CSR activities of companies

- Some of the common choices of students at the undergraduate level are Psychology, English, Economics, Political Science, History and Sociology. Subjects like Political Science, Economics and Sociology are extremely dynamic and experiential, requiring students to draw on their practical knowledge of state and society. Philosophy helps to build a critical and rational approach to life in general as it teaches basic thinking patterns.

- Political Science can be a useful base for a career in social work, human rights, social and political research and analysis, urban planning. It can also form a strong knowledge base for the Union and State Public Service Examinations and Staff Selection Commission or for the MBA entrance examination.

- Some upcoming choices are Communication and Media Studies, Journalism, Law, Gender Studies, Human Rights, Anthropology etc.
- There are various work areas available, such as: report writing, research, market surveys, workshop/event organisation, public relations, using social media networks for marketing, strategic thinking, change management etc.
- There is also a great scope in research areas like official think tanks, knowledge hubs.
- Community work - Many avenues are available in community work like community based worker, field staff, back-end workers etc. Additional supplementary skills add to the resume and thus to the job areas.

The following section of this chapter discusses educational and career opportunities in some subjects in detail:

25.1

Mathematics

India has a long and ancient mathematical tradition. India has given the world the decimal place value system, the modern way of writing numbers, and above all, the number 'zero.' Similarly, Pythagoras Theorem, an approximation to the value of 'pi', and the ratio of the circumference of a circle to its diameter were also discovered in India. It is indeed possible to build a perfectly satisfying career in mathematics (and much of this applies to other pure sciences as well) if one is deeply interested in the subject.

Careers in Mathematics: Apart from teaching, there are various other careers possible in Mathematics.

- **Government** departments engaged in space research (the Indian Space Research Organisation, or ISRO), defence research (Defence Research and Development Organisation, or DRDO), aeronautical research (National Aeronautics Limited, or NAL), all employ mathematicians to solve their special problems
- **Cryptology:** It is a system ensuring the safety of a credit card transaction and it is based on some very sophisticated mathematics. The advent of IT enabled services like E-Commerce has given a great boost to Cryptology.
- **Financial** mathematics is another area that leads to well-paid jobs.

- **Computer** giants such as IBM and Microsoft have research departments, which hire either mathematicians or theoretical computer scientists.

- **Operations Research Analysts:** It is as an interdisciplinary branch of applied mathematics and formal science that uses advanced analytical methods such as mathematical modelling, statistical analysis, and mathematical optimisation to arrive at optimal or near-optimal solutions to complex decision-making problems. It helps to make better decisions and solve problems.

- Many reputed government recognised institutes and the IITs offer graduate and PhD degrees in Mathematics. Some of these institutes also offer an undergraduate degree. Hence those who are very sure that they want to pursue a career in Mathematics can choose a path right after 12th standard. A list of such institutes is given below in table 25.1 &2.

25.2

Statistics

Statistics is the study of the collection, analysis, interpretation, presentation, and organisation of data. Statistics is a decision-making tool. Knowledge of this discipline is required everywhere from media houses to any scientist's lab. Statistics deals with uncertainty, they make you understand numbers.

Careers in Statistics: There are many job opportunities after a postgraduate degree in the discipline.

- One can opt for analytics, finance, actuarial science, software development and many more options.
- In the government sector, postgraduates can apply for positions in the Indian Statistical Service (ISS), Subordinate Statistical Service (SSS), the ministry of statistics and programme implementation.
- Banking and statistical software development.

There are many institutes in India offering specialised and integrated courses in Mathematics. These institutes include the IITs, IISERs, Tata Institute of Fundamental Research (TIFR) Harish Chandra Research Institute (HRI), Allahabad. Majority of the courses are at the Masters level, MA/MSC, Integrated PhD or Postgraduate Diplomas.

The main institutes offering undergraduate Courses in Mathematics and Statistics are:

Table 25.1&2

#	Institute	Course	Eligibility and Admission
1	Indian Statistical Institute[72] at Kolkata	3-year B. Stat. (Hons.)	12th standard from a recognised board with Math & English as subjects of study + two written tests comprising of (i) multiple choice questions & (ii) descriptive questions in Mathematics
2	Indian Statistical Institute at Bangalore	3-year B.Math. (Hons.)	
3	Chennai Mathematics Institute[73]	3-year B.Sc. (Honours) in Mathematics & Computer Science	12th standard from a recognised board + entrance test
4		3-year B.Sc. (Honours) in Mathematics & Physics	

---

[72] http://www.isical.ac.in
[73] http://www.cmi.ac.in

25.3

Economics

Economics is a social science that studies the production, consumption and distribution of goods and services, with an aim of explaining how economies work and how their agents interact. Economics includes the study of labor, land, and investments, of money, income, and production, and of taxes and government expenditures. Although labeled a "social science", modern economics is in fact often very quantitative and heavily math-oriented in practice.

The main goal of an economist is to design and develop activities through research that will help to obtain optimum benefit by allocating resources like raw materials, land, capital, technology and labour. To do this, the economists monitor and analyse demands and supply, exchange rates, business trends, taxation, employment rates, inflation, and costs of materials and find trends and develop predictions.

Application of Economics:

- Economists aim to understand how consumers and producers react to changing conditions through research, and their research findings can provide powerful guidance and influence to policy-making at the national level.
- A nation is able to make different policy decisions about taxation, regulation, and government spending as per the analysis and advice given by the economists.

- Economics can also help investors understand the potential bifurcations of national policy and their impact on companies, stocks, markets etc.

Globalisation and consequent merging of world economy has widened the career prospects for economics students in business, education, government, and the non-profit sector.

Career Prospects:

- A graduate in Economics can begin their career with entry-level jobs in banking, finance, insurance, stock markets, sales and marketing as well as corporations like consulting firms or government departments.
- They can also begin their career with government enterprises, public undertakings, investment firms, business journals and newspapers. The Indian Economics Services and Reserve Bank of India are also excellent options open to those who want to join government services (provided they have cleared the Banking exam and the interview process).
- Those who wish to pursue higher education, there are different courses at Masters and doctoral level, such as MA, M.Sc, MBA etc. and M.Phil. and a PhD and work as an analyst in the public or private sector or as a consultant. Those who wish to diversify can think of doing journalism, Law is a certification in Finance such as Certified Financial Analyst (CFA).

Education:

Economics is offered in the faculty of Arts & Humanities as well as in the faculty of Commerce at undergraduate level and then pursue a Masters and Doctoral degree later. Another option is to opt for a Liberal Arts Course (more about this, later in this chapter) with Economics as major and supporting subjects in Business and Finance. Some institutes such as University of Delhi or S.P. Jain also give an undergraduate specific degree in Economics. The list below gives a list of institutes offering a specific degree in Economics:

Table 25.3.1

#	Institute	Course	Admission
1	University of Delhi[74]	3-year Bachelor of Business Economics (BBE)	(10+2)+ English + Mathematics + any two subjects from Arts / Science / Commerce stream + 50% aggregate marks + Entrance Test
2	S.P.Jain School of Global Management [75]	3-year Bachelor of Economics (BEC)	(10+2) in ANY stream + SP Jain Entrance test (SPJET) or Scholastic Aptitude Test (SAT)
3	Christ University, Bengaluru[76]	3-year Bachelor of Arts with Triple Major**	(10+2) in ANY stream + Christ University Entrance test
4	Symbiosis School of Economics[77]	3-year Bachelor of Science in Economics (B.Sc. Economics)	(10+2) in ANY stream + Symbiosis Entrance test (SET)

---

[74] http://www.du.ac.in/du/index.php?page=business-economics
[75] http://www.spjain.org/bec/index.aspx
[76] http://www.christuniversity.in/economics/programmes
[77] http://sse.ac.in/

** **Christ University**: Following combinations of subjects are available in the triple major course. In addition, the university also offers BA in Economics as a single major.

- Bachelor of Arts (BA) in Psychology, Sociology, Economics (PSEco)
- Bachelor of Arts (BA) in Economics, Politics, Sociology (EPS)
- Bachelor of Arts (BA) in History, Economics, Politics (HEP)
- Bachelor of Science (B.Sc) Economics, Mathematics, Statistics (EMS)
- Bachelor of Arts (BA) Honours in Economics

Difference between Economics and Finance:

Finance and economics are often taught as separate subjects, but they are interrelated disciplines that influence one another in many ways. Students are often get confused while making a decision about which course to choose. Any path, especially the Economics path, supported by a certification in finance may lead to a career as an Economist, Financial Analyst or a Business or Political Analyst depending on the supporting subjects chosen in the undergraduate course. The following table shows how they are interrelated.

Economics	Finance
Social science that studies production, consumption, distribution of goods and services, inflation, recession and supply & demand relation.	Finance is an offshoot of Economics. Individuals with Economics background can make a good career in Finance
Explains the taxation and spendings of a government. It deals with forecasting growth, inflation, inflation rates etc that impact the economy of a country.	Finance encompasses the study of prices, interest rates, money flows and financial markets. It deals with study of prices, interest rates, cash flows, loan pricing, investment and insurance products
The basic core is research, analysis and forecasting	The basic core is research, analysis and forecasting
Economics is more concerned with the big picture, such as how a country is doing and will do	Finance focuses on companies, industries and the investor

25.4

Psychology

Psychology is the scientific study of the mind and behaviour. Psychology is a multifaceted discipline and includes many sub-fields of study, such areas as human development, sports, health, clinical, social behaviour, and cognitive processes. Being a science, psychology attempts to investigate the causes of behaviour using systematic and objective procedures for observation, measurement and analysis, backed-up by theoretical interpretations, generalisations, explanations and predictions.

Please note: Psychologists are different from psychiatrists; psychiatrists are MBBS doctors who have done a post-graduation in Psychiatry. They are authorised to prescribe medicines, while psychologists are NOT. Psychiatrists treat patients and psychologists help their clients with coping skills. Psychologists study a person's reactions, emotions, and behaviour, and apply their understanding of that behaviour to treat the associated behavioural problems. Treatment is focused on therapy and counselling, rather than prescribing medications for a "quick fix."

Psychologists are therefore responsible for identifying psychological, emotional, and/or behavioural issues, as well as diagnosing any specific disorders, by using information collected from patient interviews, patient's tests and records, and medical reference materials. It is also the psychologist's job to come up with an individualized treatment plan for each patient, and to modify it as necessary over time (depending on the patient's progress).

Career avenues in Psychology: Although both the fields are related to psychology, being a psychiatrist and being a psychologist mean different things; the career prospects too vary accordingly.

To become a Psychiatrist: Any student who wishes to become a psychiatrist has to first get an MBBS degree. After that, there are three options available.

- o A student may complete a 3-year MD in Psychiatric Medicine.
- o A student may get a Diploma in Psychiatric Medicine (DPM).
- o A student may get a DNB Psychiatric Medicine from National Board of Examinations

Career Avenues:

- Hospitals, Mental hospitals
- De-addiction
- Private Practice as a Psychiatrist
- Employment as a teacher and consultant in Medical Colleges

Further education such as post-doctoral fellowships, Fellowships, Super-speciality courses like Doctor of Medicine (DM) in Psychiatric medicine is available in National Institute of Mental Health and Neurosciences (**NIMHANS**)[78] and

---

[78] http://nimhans.ac.in

Topiwala National Medical College and B. Y. L. Nair Charitable Hospital, Mumbai (**TNMC**)[79].

To become a Psychologist: a student needs to complete 12th standard, preferably with Psychology as one of the subjects in 11th and 12th standard and complete a Bachelor of Arts (BA) with Psychology as major or honours. Generally the curriculum of psychology honours focuses on personality theories, development theories, psychotherapy, stress management etc.

For further education, one can complete a master's degree in Psychology and then a Doctorate (PhD). The postgraduate and doctoral programs focus their studies more on research, which is great for pursuing either a research or teaching job. The graduate degrees emphasise practice, such as counselling. A Bachelor's degree and/or a PG Diploma in Counselling is a good combination to start independent practice as a counsellor for adults, or children, or take a job in schools, companies, colleges etc. as a counsellor.

Tata Institute of Social Sciences (TISS)[80] **offers two masters courses:**

1. MA in Applied Psychology with specialisation in Counselling Psychology
2. MA in Applied Psychology with specialisation in Clinical Psychology

---

[79] http://www.tnmcnair.com
[80] http://www.tiss.edu

Fergusson College, Pune also offers different courses in psychology, they are:

1. MA Industrial Psychology
2. MA Clinical Psychology
3. PG Course in Counseling Psychology (PGCCP - autonomous course)

For more details the website of Fergusson College[81], Pune.

Applied Psychology:

Applied psychology is the use of psychological methods and findings of scientific psychology to solve practical problems of human and animal behaviour and experience. Mental health, organisational psychology, business management, education, health, product design, ergonomics, and law are just a few of the areas that have been influenced by the application of psychological principles and findings. Some of the areas of applied psychology include clinical psychology, counselling psychology, evolutionary psychology, industrial and organisational psychology, legal psychology, neuropsychology, occupational health psychology, human factors, forensic psychology, engineering psychology, school psychology, sports psychology, traffic psychology, community psychology, medical psychology.

---

[81] http://www.fergusson.edu

Career avenues in psychology can be divided into two broad areas:

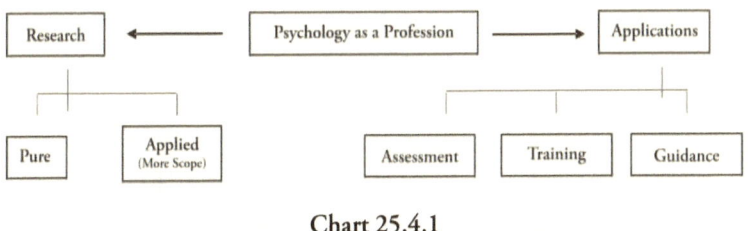

Chart 25.4.1

The different specialisations in psychology are:

- **Clinical Psychology:** Clinical psychologists assess and treat people with psychological problems. They may act as therapists for people who are experiencing normal psychological crises (e.g., grief) or for individuals suffering from chronic psychiatric disorders.

- **Counselling Psychology:** Counselling psychologists work in a similar manner as the clinical psychologists. However, they tend to focus more on persons with adjustment problems rather than on persons suffering from severe psychological disorders. They may be trained in psychology departments or in education departments. Counselling psychologists are employed in academic settings, college counselling centres, community mental health centres.

- **Health Psychology:** Health psychologists are concerned with psychology's contributions to the promotion and maintenance of good health and the prevention and treatment of illness. They may design and conduct programmes to help individuals stop smoking, lose weight, shed alcoholism, manage stress, and stay physically fit. They are employed in hospitals, medical schools, rehabilitation centres, public health agencies, academic settings, and private practice.

- **Teaching and Research**: Opportunities are available in colleges, university departments, government agencies such as Centres for Disease Control or in private research organisations.

- **Industrial / Organisational Psychology**: These psychologists are concerned with the relationships between people and their work environments. They are employed in business, government agencies, factories, industrial set-ups corporate houses and academic establishments.

- **Sports Psychology**: Sports psychologists are concerned with the psychological factors that improve athletic performance. Sports psychologists typically work in academic settings and/or as consultants for sports teams.

- **Community Counselling**: These psychologists work in human service agencies in the local community - for example, in community mental health centres. They are trained in administering various types of psychological test such as aptitude tests, personality tests etc.

- **Educational Psychology**: Educational psychologists attempt to understand the basic aspects of human learning and to develop materials and strategies for enhancing the learning process. Educational psychologists are typically trained in departments of education (known as departments of psychology) and employed in colleges and universities.

- **School Counselling**: School counsellors work with children who are troubled, helping such children function more effectively with their peers and teachers, deal with family problems, etc. They work at the elementary, middle, and high school levels.

- **Social Work:** Social workers who practice psychotherapy are usually called either clinical social workers or psychiatric social workers. Clinical social workers are trained to diagnose and treat psychological problems. Psychiatric social workers provide services to individuals, married couples, families, and small groups. They work in mental health centres, counselling centres, sheltered workshops, hospitals, and schools.

- **Criminal Psychology:** Criminal psychology, also referred to as criminological psychology, is the study of the wills, thoughts, intentions, and reactions of criminals and all aspects in the criminal behaviour. A criminal psychologist assesses the mind-set of an individual who has committed a crime and prepares a written psychological report. A criminal psychologist must also be familiar with laws concerning mental health and criminal behaviour. Currently this specialisation is not available in India.

Good life is a process, not a state of being...
It is a direction, not a destination...

-Carl Rogers (American Psychologist)

□□□

25.5

Foreign Languages

We live in an increasingly globalised world and companies are constantly expanding overseas and dealing with clients from all over the world. With Indian companies emerging as global players and Indian market being eyed by multinational companies, it becomes essential that there is no dearth of professionals who can overcome language barriers and facilitate smooth communication for proper business transactions. Foreign language experts with a good understanding of cultures are in great demand in the corporate world. The scope of foreign languages as career is stupendous and candidates willing to explore it have multitude of job opportunities in various multinational companies and multilateral organisations. Moreover, language skills are essential attribute in most professions and help in the advancement of career.

Education:

- There are various options to learn foreign languages.
- Several students start learning a foreign language in their schools, there are numerous others who opt for it in the 11th standard or after 12th standard when they join the bachelors course to gain a Bachelor's degree (BA) in a particular foreign language.
- But apart from a degree, there are different certificate and diploma courses which a student can pursue while pursuing a bachelors course in any other subject, for e.g. while pursuing Bachelor of Commerce (B.Com.) a

student can pursue a certificate or diploma course in French/German or Korean etc. Eligibility for such courses is generally after 12ᵗʰ standard.

- Those who are interested in higher education in a particular language complete a bachelors first in the same language and then pursue a masters or also a Ph. further.

Tips for those who want to pursue a career in Foreign Language:

- Start Early: Language skills are like sport skills, those who start early get an advantage hence begin to learn a foreign language early, at school level or latest after 10ᵗʰ standard.
- Ask the following questions before you join a course in foreign language:

  ▪ Why am I learning this?
  ▪ How much time do I have to learn?
  ▪ Do I have ample time? Will I be able to learn a totally new script?
  ▪ If I have less time, what are the languages which use Roman Script?
  ▪ What is my objective of learning this language? (How do I want to use it?) - for e.g. I plan to study in a foreign country:

  In Canada, one needs to learn French

  Singapore - Chinese, Japan - Japanese

  Going for a job in Gulf countries - Arabic

  ▪ Is it the right career for me?

186

- What would it cost me?
- Do you have a specific career goal other than a foreign language and want to learn the language as a supporting skill related to your profession? Then, you must find out about the aspired profession and select a language that will equip you with the appropriate skills. For e.g.-

- Career in Aviation - Russian/French
- Research - According to the country
- Commerce and Economics (KPO/BPO) - French, German, Italian, Spanish, Dutch, Portuguese
- Hospitality, Travel and Tourism - Any or Multiple foreign languages
- Mechanical - German
- Automobile - Japanese/Korean
- Interpreter - Any languages, but more opportunities are available in Delhi
- What are the opportunities available? - For e.g. - Spanish - The largest spoken language - globally, French - Aviation, IT, Automobile, Japanese - Automobile, ITs

Some professions where a foreign language expert can work:

- Diplomatic Service Professional
- Foreign Language Trainer
- Translator for MNCs and Government Organisations
- Research Associate
- Interpreter
- Tourist Guide/Hospitality Industry
- Air Hostess or Flight Steward

- Freelance Writer, Translator, Interpreter
- Public Relation Officer
- KPO (Knowledge Process Outsourcing) and BPO (Business Process Outsourcing)

Institutes offering course in Foreign Languages:

Table 25.5.1

#	Institute	Courses	Languages
1	School of Language and Literature, Jawaharlal Nehru University[82], New Delhi	Bachelors/ Masters/ Doctorate / Certificate	Arabic, African, German, Chinese, South East Asian, French, German, Japanese, Korean, Persian, Russian, Spanish, Portuguese, Latin American
2	Department of Foreign Languages, University of Pune[83]	Bachelors/ Masters/ PhD/Dipl oma/Certi ficate	German, Russian, Spanish, French, Japanese
3	Alliance Français[84]	Certificate	French

[82] http://www.jnu.ac.in/SLLCS
[83] http://www.unipune.ac.in/dept/fine_arts/foreign_languages
[84] http://www.afindia.org

4	Goethe-Institut - Max Mueller Bhavan[85]	Certificate	German
5	Instituto Hispania[86]	Certificate	Spanish
6	Symbiosis Institute of Foreign & Indian Languages (SIFIL)	Certificate	Chinese, French, German, Japanese, Spanish, Korean

❑❑❑

---

[85] http://www.goethe.de
[86] http://www.institutohispania.com
[86] http://www.sifil-symbiosis.org/courses.html

26

Liberal Arts

A liberal arts degree program is interdisciplinary, covering topics within the humanities, as well as social, natural and formal sciences. A student has to choose a group of subjects out of which s/he has to choose a major at a later stage. The choice of subjects available may differ in different institutions. However the general spectrum of the liberal art covers the following fields:

- Humanities: Include art, literature, linguistics, philosophy, religion, ethics, modern foreign languages, music, theatre, speech, classical languages etc.
- Social Sciences: include history, psychology, law, sociology, politics, gender studies, anthropology, economics, geography, business informatics etc.
- Natural Sciences: include astronomy, biology, chemistry, physics, botany, zoology, archaeology, geology, Earth sciences etc.
- Formal Sciences: include mathematics, logic, statistics, Computer Science, Information theory, Game theory, Systems theory, decision theory etc.

In general, the term liberal arts refer to degree programs that aim at providing a broader spectrum of knowledge and skills. It seeks to form a broad foundation of knowledge that can be used in a wide spectrum of careers. Students of the Liberal Arts Course learn to think critically, examine the world around them, communicate effectively and adjust to changing situations.

Skills gained from a Liberal Arts Curriculum:

- Analytical, evaluative, critical and creative thinking skills
- Effective oral and written communication skills
- Problem-solving and observation skills
- Ability to synthesise and apply new ideas
- Experience in quantitative and qualitative data analysis
- Critical and reflective reading skills
- Numerical skills
- Research ability
- Organisation, time-management, decision-making and team skills
- Self-directed learning ability
- Foreign language skills and cross-cultural knowledge

A student has to choose a group of interdisciplinary subjects out of which s/he has to choose a major at a later stage. The degree awarded is Bachelor of Art (BA) or Bachelor of Science (B.Sc.) depending on which faculty the major belongs to. For e.g. if the major is in Economics, Business Studies, Media Studies, Sociology, English, Psychology etc. then the degree awarded will be BA. Those graduating with majors like Mathematics, Biology, Computer Science etc., the degree awarded will be B.Sc.

Benefits of a liberal arts degree:

- Students gain strong foundation knowledge in a wider range of subjects. This enables them to make more informed decision in choosing a preferred career path.
- Liberal arts degree is known to instil transferable skills, which help in quickly adapting to a changing workplace. Hence it has started getting more and more preference from the employers.
- Provides a foundation for further studies as the undergraduates have developed a broader perspective and an ability to learn across diverse fields of studies.

Careers with a liberal arts degree:

A wide variety of careers are available to students who complete a Liberal Studies degree. These can be in business, government, and social service agencies like adult and family services, criminal justice, and health and welfare depending on the major. The liberal arts degree prepares the students in various careers or for further education in different areas like:

- Editor, Journalist, Publicist
- Entry-level Management Personnel
- Social Services, Human Relations, Public Relations
- Analyst, IT/ITES
- Creative, Technical writer, Copywriter
- Psychologist, counsellor
- Communication
- Law
- History and Anthropology
- Banking, Financial Services and Insurance, E-Commerce

- Media and Advertisement
- Healthcare
- Education

Slowly students and parents are getting aware of the Liberal Arts Education and its benefits. Currently there are a few schools offering a degree in Liberal Arts. Some of them are mentioned below:

Table 26.1

Institute	Program	Place
Flame University[87]	3-year BA/ BSc/ BBA	Pune
Symbiosis School of Liberal Arts[88]	3-year BA / BSc	Pune
Ashoka University[89]	4-year BA / BSc	New Delhi

Eligibility and Admission Process:

- The eligibility for the Liberal Arts Courses in India is 12th standard pass or appearing.
- Entrance Test: Some of the institutes conduct their own Entrance Test (Symbiosis School of Liberal Arts) or some school consider score of the SAT (Scholastic Aptitude Test) or ACT (American College Testing)* Details of SAT and ACT are given in the chapter on Overseas Education

---

[87] http://www.flame.edu.in
[88] http://www.ssla.edu.in
[89] http://www.ashoka.edu.in

- The admission procedure usually includes review of application and the supporting documents may include an essay on a given essay topic or a prompt.

27
Teacher Education

According to UNESCO (2005), teacher education "addresses environmental, social, and economic contexts to create locally relevant and culturally appropriate teacher education programmes for both pre-service and in-service teachers." Teacher education generally includes four elements: improving the general educational background of the trainee teachers; increasing their knowledge and understanding of the subjects they are to teach; pedagogy and understanding of children and learning; and the development of practical skills and competences. Teacher Education Institutions have the potential to bring changes within educational systems that will shape the knowledge and skills of future generations.

The National Council for Teacher Education (NCTE)[90], is a statutory body of Government of India which recognises and regulates all Teacher Education Programs in India. There are courses at the diploma, bachelors, masters and doctorate level offered by various universities across the country. They are:

a. Diploma in early childhood education programme leading to Diploma in Preschool Education (DPSE)
b. 2-year Elementary teacher education programme leading to Diploma in Elementary Education (D.El.Ed.).

---

[90] http://ncte-india.org

c. Bachelor of elementary teacher education programme leading to Bachelor of Elementary Education (B.El.Ed.) degree.

d. Bachelor of education programme leading to Bachelor of Education (B.Ed.) degree.

e. Master of education programme leading to Master of Education (M.Ed.) degree.

f. Diploma in physical education programme leading to Diploma in Physical Education (D.P.Ed.).

g. Bachelor of physical education programme leading to Bachelor of Physical Education (B.P.Ed.) degree.

h. Master of physical education programme leading to Master of Physical Education (M.P.Ed.) degree.

i. Diploma in elementary education programme through Open and Distance Learning System leading to Diploma in Elementary Education (D.El.Ed.).

j. Bachelor of education programme through Open and Distance Learning System leading to Bachelor of Education (B.Ed.) degree.

k. Diploma in arts education (Visual Arts) programme leading to Diploma in Arts Education (Visual Arts).

l. Diploma in arts education (Performing Arts) programme leading to Diploma in Arts Education (Performing Arts).

m. 4-year integrated programme leading to B.A.B.Ed./B.Sc.B.Ed. degree.

n. Bachelor of education programme 3-year (Part Time) leading to Bachelor of Education (B.Ed) degree.

o. 3-year integrated programme leading to B.Ed., M.Ed (Integrated) degree.

Diploma in Elementary Education (D.El.Ed):

It is a 2-year professional program of teacher education which aims to prepare teachers for the elementary state of education i.e. standards 1st to 8th.

Eligibility: Candidates with at least 50% marks in the higher secondary 12th standard or its equivalent examination are eligible for admission.

Admission Procedure: Admission is made on merit on the basis of marks obtained in the qualifying examination and/or in the entrance examination or any other selection process as per the policy of the State Government /UT Administration.

Bachelor in Education (B.Ed.): Course Duration 2 years for 2015

NCTE Norms for B.Ed. for 2015 and Course Duration 2-years: The Bachelor of Education programme, generally known as B.Ed., is a professional course that prepares teachers for upper primary or middle level (classes VI-VIII), secondary level (classes IX-X) and senior secondary level (classes XI-XII). The programme shall be offered in composite institutions as defined in clause (b) of regulations 2

Duration: The B.Ed. programme is of 2-year, which can be completed in a maximum of three years from the date of admission to the programme.

Eligibility:

(a) Candidates with at least 50% marks either in the **Bachelor's Degree** and/or in the Master's Degree in Sciences/Social Sciences/Humanity, Bachelor's in

Engineering or Technology with specialisation in Science and Mathematics with 55% marks or any other qualification equivalent thereto, are eligible for admission to the programme.

Admission Procedure:

Admission shall be made on merit on the basis of marks obtained in the qualifying examination and/or in the entrance examination or any other selection process as per the policy of the State and the respective universities.

Curriculum:

The B.Ed. curriculum is designed to integrate the study of subject knowledge, human development, pedagogical knowledge and communication skills and contains three broad curricular areas: Perspectives in Education, Curriculum and Pedagogic Studies, and Engagement with the Field.

D.Ed. – Teacher Training Courses:

The Diploma in Education (D.Ed.) is of 2-year duration. It is a training program for those who want to work in the kindergarten (pre-primary) schools. The course provides knowledge regarding a number of aspects of education like language, education policy, literacy, curriculum and information technology.

Eligibility: 12ᵗʰ standard from a recognised board + Common Entrance Test conducted by Maharashtra State

Council of Education Research and Training (MSCERT)[91], in Maharashtra.

Admission Process: Date of the Common Entrance Test is announced by M.Sc. ERT after the 12th standard results are out. Admission is given through the collective merit of the entrance test and 12th standard aggregate marks.

> It is the supreme art of the teacher to awaken joy in creative expression and knowledge.
>
> -Albert Einstein

❑❑❑

---

[91] http://www.mscert.org.in

Creative Careers

28

Art and Design

Now days, people are talking a lot about careers in Design and Art. Many students get confused about these two terms and face difficulty in choosing the right path. Let us first try to understand these two terms and the similarities and differences between them.

What separate Art from Design, where does one end and the other start, how do you demarcate the two – this has been debated for a long time. Artists and designers both create visual compositions using a shared knowledge base; in this aspect, the two fields are quite similar. However, the purpose or aim, or the final output of both the subjects are entirely different.

Art:

Art is a diverse range of human activities, which create visual, auditory, or performing artworks that express the artist's imaginative or technical skill; the intention behind creating these artworks is to express oneself, and they are to be appreciated for their beauty, creativity and the emotions expressed through them. These artworks are chiefly called 'creative art' or 'fine art'. The oldest form of art is visual arts, which include painting, sculpture, printmaking, photography, and other visual media. Music, theatre, film, dance, and other performing arts, as well as literature are also included in the arts. Works of art can tell stories or simply express an aesthetic truth or feeling. Visual art is appreciated primarily for its imaginative, aesthetic, or intellectual content. Art need not cater to the consumer, and this is the main distinction between art and design. The main focus of the Art is to communicate feelings, emotions, social or cultural messages etc. to educate, motivate or to simply entertain; while Design, will always cater to an end-user or customer.

Design:

Design may be defined as an activity that translates an idea into a 'blueprint', which can be used to create or manufacture something useful. For example an Interior Designer or a Product Designer designs a home or a car respectively, both of which have a definitive use. Similarly a graphic designer will design certain graphics to be used in a book, brochure or a website. Scientists can invent technologies, manufacturers can make products, engineers can make them function and marketers can sell them, but only designers can combine insight into all these things and turn a concept into something that's desirable, viable, commercially successful and adds value to people's lives.

Design is need based; a design that has no specific 'use' is not a good design. A fashion designer may design a beautiful, wonderful dress; however, if it is not practical, or cannot be worn (in short, if the design has no 'use'), it will be rejected by the user. One cannot make a design for its sake, the way one can make art for its sake.

The following table will further illustrate the differences between 'art' and 'design', and help give you a clear idea about the two fields.

Art	Design
Asking questions to challenge the user. For e.g. A painting/photograph showing hazards of too much use of a mobile phone	Providing solutions/address the need of the user. For e.g. to design a smaller, lighter mobile phone handset
Art inspires - looking at some painting/listening to a song may inspire you.	The main goal of design is to be useful, inspiration might sometimes be supplementary
Art is unique, it cannot be replicated. There is no plan while creating it. It simply comes from the artist's imagination and thoughts. Thus it has no rules.	There are rules in Design. Even if it is not beautiful, it has to be useful and solve problems. Thus the rules will provide answers for questions like Why? For what? etc.
Art is a natural talent (ability), the artist is born with it which can be further cultivated with proper training and practice	Design is a skill, which can be acquired with appropriate training and practice. (You do not have to be a great artist to be a designer)

❑❑❑

28.1

Architecture

Architecture is the process of planning, designing, and constructing buildings and other non-building structures like bridges, towers, canals, dams, arenas, stadiums, roads etc. It includes planning and designing of different forms, spaces and ambiences after considering their functional, technicality, aesthetic, social, cultural and environmental aspects.

Architecture is included in the Engineering faculty and the All India Council of Technical Education (AICTE) approves the Architecture Courses because Architecture is closely related to Civil Engineering. They both are involved in the preparation and the creation of structures and work alongside one another when designing a construction project. The Architect provides the design with proper arrangements for ventilation, lighting, room and facility arrangement, dwelling space and land utilisation; the Civil Engineer is involved in the implementation of the design, supervision of construction, and maintains the quality of work. Thus the Architect takes lead on design and the Civil Engineer concentrates on the physics of the project.

Career scope of an Architect:

- Planning, designing and constructing a physical indoors or outdoors structure (buildings, bridges, dams, environment etc.). Architects are responsible for designing these places.

- Discussing the objectives, requirements, and budget of a project with clients.
- Provide various predesign services, such as feasibility and environmental impact studies, site selection, cost analyses, and design requirements.
- Develop final construction plans showing the appearance of the structure to be built and details of its construction.
- Preparing drawings of the structural system; air-conditioning, heating, and ventilating systems; electrical systems; communications systems; and plumbing.
- Preparing landscape plans.
- The scope is not limited to this. The Architect can diversify as an Interior or Industrial Designer after completing the bachelor's degree. Similarly, the architect can specialise in the different related areas like Landscape Architecture or Sustainable Design.

Current Scenario:

Infrastructure Design and development is the need of the day in India. Architects will be leaders in this field. While other professionals are narrowing their scope and going into specialisations, Architects are broadening their horizons, working on a multitude of projects in different areas.

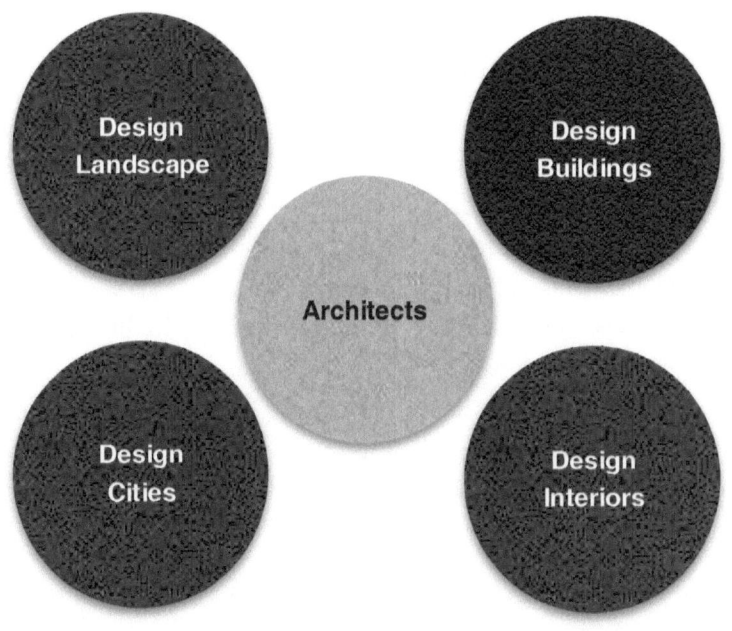

Education:

The Architecture education in India is governed by the Council of Architecture (COA)[92]. The COA prescribes 5-year **Bachelor of Architecture (B.Arch.)** degree as an undergraduate degree. There are about 481 institutes in India imparting the B.Arch. degree. These include constituent colleges/departments of universities, deemed universities, affiliated colleges/schools, IITs, NITs and autonomous institutions. Out of these, about 76 Institutes are in Maharashtra.

---

[92] http://www.coa.gov.in

Admission Process:

A. Through JEE Main:

The Centrally Funded Technical Institutes like IITs, NITs and School of Planning offer Bachelor of Architecture programme. Similarly Birla Institute of Technology at Mesra, (**BITS, Mesra-Ranchi**)[93], also offers the B. Arch programme. Admissions to these are given on the basis of marks obtained in Paper 2 of JEE Main. The Paper-2 of JEE Main contains three parts: Mathematics, Aptitude Test, and Drawing Test. It is conducted on the same day when the Paper -1 is conducted but in the second half at all exam centres. List of the Centrally Funded Technical Institutes offering B.Arch. degree through JEE Main:

#	Institute	#	Institute
1	IIT Rourke[94]	8	National Institute of Technology, Patna[95]
2	IIT Kharagpur[96]	9	National Institute of Technology, Raipur
3	Maulana Azad National Institute of Technology, Bhopal[97]	10	National Institute of Technology, Rourkela[98]

[93] https://www.bitmesra.ac.in
[94] http://www.iitr.ac.in
[95] http://www.nitp.ac.in
[96] http://www.iitkgp.ac.in
[97] http://www.manit.ac.in
[98] http://www.nitrkl.ac.in

#	Institute	#	Institute
4	National Institute of Technology, Calicut[99]	11	National Institute of Technology, Tiruchirappalli[100]
5	National Institute of Technology, Hamirpur[101]	12	School of Planning and Architecture, Bhopal[102]
6	Malaviya National Institute of Technology, Jaipur[103]	13	School of Planning and Architecture, New Delhi[104]
7	Visvesvaraya National Institute of Technology, Nagpur[105]	14	School of Planning and Architecture, Vijayawada[106]

Eligibility: Passed 12th standard examination with 50% total marks and Mathematics as compulsory subject including total five subjects. Detailed information is available on the JEE Main[107] website.

Through NATA :

The Council of Architecture (COA) conducts National Aptitude Test in Architecture (NATA) at the national level to facilitate the process of first year B.Arch. admissions. The

---

[99] http://www.nitc.ac.in
[100] http://www.nitt.edu
[101] http://www.nith.ac.in
[102] http://www.spabhopal.ac.in
[103] http://www.mnit.ac.in
[104] http://www.spa.ac.in
[105] http://vnit.ac.in
[106] http://www.spav.ac.in
[107] http://jeemain.nic.in

purpose of conducting NATA is to provide a single scheme of examination to assess the Architectural aptitude of students. It measures drawing and observations skills, sense of proportion, aesthetic sensitivity and critical thinking ability in the field of Architecture. NATA score is valid for 2 years. Candidates can attempt NATA for a maximum of five times, within two years of the first attempt. The best score out of the number of attempts (maximum 5) within two years will be considered for admission. In other words, an average of these two scores is considered for admission. Hence before, reapplying for the exam, do consider this, as if your latest score is less than the previous valid score, then due to averaging, the best score also will go down.

The test dates are available between April to May and again between June and August. A candidate has to register online for a suitable date and centre from the available option on the NATA website. The test is in two sections. The paper based section tests drawing aptitude and the computer based section tests aesthetic sensitivity.

Paper based Drawing Test: this test aims at gauging –

- Ability to sketch a given object proportionately and rendering the same in visually appealing manner.
- Visualising and drawing the effects of light on the object and shadows cast on surroundings.
- Sense of perspective drawing
- Combining and composing given three-dimensional elements to form a building or structural form.
- Creating interesting two-dimensional composition using given shapes and forms.

- Creating visual harmony using colours in given composition. Understanding of scale and proportions.
- Drawing from memory through pencil sketch on themes from day to day experiences.

Computer based Aesthetic Sensitivity Test: this test is aimed at understanding –

- Perception, imagination and observation, creativity and communication along with architectural awareness and comprises of -
- Visualising three-dimensional objects from two-dimensional drawings.
- Visualising different sides of three-dimensional objects.
- Identifying commonly used materials and objects based on their textural qualities.
- Analytical reasoning.
- Mental Ability.
- Imaginative comprehension and expression.
- Architectural awareness

Eligibility: 12th standard or equivalent examination with Mathematics as one of the subjects with minimum 50% total marks. Detailed information is available on the NATA website[108].

Admission Process in Maharashtra in other than CFTI institutes:

- **Eligibility**: 12th standard passed with minimum 50% aggregate marks + Mathematics as one of the subjects

---

[108] https://www.nata.in

OR a 3-year full time Diploma after 10ᵗʰ standard in ANY subject, recognised by AICTE / Central/State Government with minimum 50% marks AND Candidate should have obtained minimum 40% marks i.e. 80 marks out of 200 in NATA exam.

- Determination of Merit of the candidate for CAP round: Merit will be decided on the Merit Score out of total 200 marks with equal weightage (50:50) as given below:

1) NATA-2015 score: 100 Marks (The score of NATA obtained by the candidate out of 200 will be converted into marks out of 100)

2) HSC/Full time Diploma or its Equivalent examination's score: 100 Marks (Aggregate marks obtained by the candidate in HSC/Full time Diploma (10+3 level) or its Equivalent examination will be converted into marks out of 100)

- Candidate who has appeared for paper 2 of JEE Main 2015 and obtained minimum 40% marks will be assigned a provisional merit number as follows:

1) All India (JEE Main 2015) score: 100 Marks (The score of paper 2 of JEE Main 2015 obtained by the candidate will be converted into marks out of 100)

2) HSC / 3-year Full Time Diploma (after 10ᵗʰ standard) or its Equivalent examination's score. Aggregate marks obtained by the candidate in 12ᵗʰ standard / 3-year Full Time Diploma or its

Equivalent examination will be converted into marks out of 100.

Architecture is really about well-being. I think that people want to feel good in a space... On the one hand it's about shelter, but it's also about pleasure!

- Zaha Hadid (First woman architect to receive the Pritzker Architecture)

◻◻◻

28.2
Design

A designer is someone who is able to balance artistic talent and training with technical knowledge and business know-how, to meet the industry's requirements. First priority is given to create something that reaches the commercial and technical standards rather than only being a good work of art. Designers work with people of different disciplines to reach this goal.

There are a variety of Design courses available other than Architecture. These courses also focus on creating a piece of work or a plan as per the need of the user, in an artistic and creative way. Design can be a shape, a configuration or a pattern. Many courses at different levels, such as certificate, diploma, Bachelors (B. Design) or Masters Level, are available for those who want to develop a career in the Design. Designing is a vast field, and has multiple applications in different fields. Thus there are a variety of design courses available based on the application and field. The list below shows the different fields of design courses:

- Communication Design (Graphic, Animation, Web, Printing, Film and Video)
- Space Design (Architecture, Interior, Exhibition, Retail, Set Design)
- Industrial/Product Design (Transportation, Furniture, Ceramics, Product and Packaging)
- Automobile Design

- Fashion Design (Textile, Fashion, Accessory, Jewellery)
- Interaction Design (User experience design, User interface design, New media design, Game design)
- Design management (Design Policy, Design Strategy, Design Planning, Transformation Design)

The curriculum of these courses usually involves certain fundamental and certain special courses, which are based on the specialty. Generally, in any Design school, the student needs to be self-motivated because it is a creative field and one has to apply his/her thoughts, ideas and creativity. There is a one-to-one interaction with the student and the facilitator and emphasis is on learning through solving a problem.

In all design courses, be it an Architecture course or a Design course, the student learns to research, apply logical reasoning and conviction. Another expectation from the student is that s/he should be able to present and convince the idea to a client.

Details of different courses:

Duration: The Diploma courses are of 2-3 years duration. B. Design courses are for 3 or 4 years. Some institutes also offer a 5-year Integrated Masters course.

Eligibility: For the undergraduate courses is 12th standard from a recognised board in ANY stream with minimum 45% - 50% marks in 12th standard + Entrance Test

Each institution generally conducts the Entrance Test separately. For e.g. the entrance test for admissions to National Institute of Design (NID) is called National Entrance Examination for Design (NEED), National Institute of

Fashion Technology (NIFT) conduct their own test, similarly, Industrial Design Centre (IDC) at IIT Bombay conduct Undergraduate Common Entrance Examination for Design (UCEED) for their 4-year B. Design Course. Some institutes accept students qualifying in the NEED test. Many institutes also require submission of an art portfolio (samples of the work done by the candidate) and also conduct an interview after the student becomes eligible in the entrance test.

The list below gives details of the major Design Institutes in India and Maharashtra:

Table 28.2.1

#	Institute	Course	Subject	Entrance Test
1	National Institute of Design, Ahmedabad[109]	4-year B. Design	Product Design, Furniture and Interior Design, Ceramic and Glass Design, Graphic Design, Animation Film Design, Film and Video Communication, Exhibition Design, Textile and Apparel Design	NEED + Studio Test + Interview

---

[109] http://www.nid.edu

#	Institute	Course	Subject	Entrance Test
2	IDC, IIT Bombay[110]	4-year B. Design	Specialisation through selection of electives	UCEED (no studio or interview)
3	IIT Guwahati[111]	4-year B. Design	Industrial Design and Communication Design	12th standard (PCM) + JEE + Design Test
4	Indian Institute of Information Technology, Design and Manufacturing, Jabalpur (IIITDM, Jabalpur)[112]	4-year B. Design	Design	UCEED (no studio or interview)
5	National Institute of Fashion Technology, New Delhi[113]	4-year B. Design 4-year B.F. Tech	B. Design- Fashion, Leather, Accessory, Textile, Knitwear, Fashion Communication B.F. Tech - Apparel Production	NIFT All India Examination + Studio Test + Interview

---

[110] http://www.iitb.ac.in/uceed/2016
[111] http://www.iitg.ac.in
[112] http://design.iiitdmj.ac.in
[113] http://www.nift.ac.in

#	Institute	Course	Subject	Entrance Test
6	MAEER's MIT Institute of Design, Pune[114]	4.5-year Graduate Diploma	Product Design, Interior Space and Equipment Design, Transportation Design, Display and Events Design, Graphic Design. Animation Design, Fashion Design and Film and Video Design	MAEER's All India Exam + Studio Test + Interview
7	Srishti School of Design, Bangalore[115]	4-year B. Design	Business Service and Systems, Human Centred Design, Industrial Art and Design Practices, Information Arts and Information Design Practices, Public Space Design, Visual Communication and Strategic Branding	Srishti Entrance and Aptitude Test (SEAT) + Portfolio Review + Interview

---

[114] http://www.mitid.edu.in
[115] http://srishti.ac.in

217

#	Institute	Course	Subject	Entrance Test
8	Srishti School of Design, Bangalore	4-year B.Cr.A. (Creative Arts)	Contemporary Art Practice, Creative Writing, Digital Media Arts, Experimental Media Arts, Film	Same as # 7
9	Indian School of Design and Education in collaboration with Parsons, New York[116]	1+3-year UG Diploma	Communication Design, Fashion Design, Interior Design, Product Design	ISDI Challenge (Entrance Test) + Portfolio review
10	Symbiosis Institute of Design[117]	4-year B. Design	Communication Design, Industrial Design, Fashion Communication, Fashion Design	Symbiosis Entrance Test (SET) + Studio Test + Interview
11	National Institute of Technology, Rourkela[118]	4-year B.Tech	Industrial Design	JEE

---

[116] http://www.isdi.in
[117] http://sid.edu.in
[118] http://nitrkl.ac.in

#	Institute	Course	Subject	Entrance Test
12	DSK International School of Design[119]	5-year Integrated Masters	Digital Management with specialisation in Product, Transportation, Digital Design Animation Design Fashion Design Video Game Design	Written Test + Drawing Test+ Creative Test + Interview

Career Prospects:

Design graduates can work as independent professionals; they can set up their own design studio or firm or they can take a job. The product and industrial designers usually work in a manufacturing, production company or design studios. Communication and interaction designers work in fields like media industry, publishing and advertisement firms, and now, even in the IT industry. With a few years of experience, designers then have opportunities to get into design management and R&D.

A designer needs to be a sensitive human being. He should be able to integrate his ideas and creativity into a product as per the need of the user, which is also commercially successful.

---

[119] http://dskic.in

29

Fine Art and Performing Art

Fine Art or Visual Arts includes subjects like drawing, painting, textile design, sculpting, pottery, interior design, printmaking, photography, and the performing arts like music, dance, drama, music etc. It is essentially an art form, which primarily focuses on creating forms on the basis of concepts, and ideas, keeping in mind the aesthetic value and its beauty rather than its use. It deals with the passion of a person. One who achieves expertise in any of the fine arts can be called an artist.

A relatively new area - commercial art - is the application of the different types of art media for commercial purposes, such as creating work paintings (e.g. murals, portraits, landscapes etc.), sculpting statues, monuments or creating advertisements, billboards, book jackets, window displays, cinema slides, technical catalogues, packaging etc. Someone joining this field would not only need to be a good artist but also be adept in the 'art of marketing and publicity.

> Painting is poetry that is seen rather than felt, and poetry is painting that is felt rather than seen...
>
> -Leonardo da Vinci

Education:

Fine Arts: There are a large number of Fine Arts/Commercial Arts courses offered at the certificate; diploma and degree level at a number of institutions all over India. Duration of the certificate or diploma courses ranges between 1 to 4 years. Many institutes also offer an undergraduate degree course called Bachelor of Fine Arts (B.F.A.). The B.F.A. degree is often given in one specialty for e.g. B.F.A. in Painting/ Sculpture/ Ceramics/Textile Design/Interior Decoration etc. The B.F.A. courses are of either 3 or 4-year duration.

The main objectives of the Fine Arts courses are:

- To offer creative and practical skills of the students and develop them as artists.
- Learn interdisciplinary collaboration

Directorate of Art, Maharashtra State, Mumbai:

With the idea of increasing high quality opportunities for arts learning in both, former and informal setting and to increase the accessibility to a variety of arts education disciplines, and to expand the number of institutes providing education in Fine Arts, Government of Maharashtra has established the Directorate of Art, which authorises the syllabi of all the Government aided institutes in Maharashtra State. A list of these colleges and their courses is given in table 29.1 Entry to the undergraduate courses offered by these institutes is through the Entrance Test (**MH-AAC-CET**) conducted by Directorate of Art, Maharashtra State (DOA)[120].

DOA Entrance Test (MH-AAC-CET) Eligibility:

- 12th standard pass with minimum 45% marks aggregate from ANY stream, and with English as a compulsory subject.
- Test is for 100 marks and contains 4 papers - Object Drawing, Design Practical, Memory Drawing, Written test based on Art and Design
- If the candidate has passed Intermediate Drawing Examination conducted by the Maharashtra Government, S/he gets 2 to 5 marks extra depending on the grade received in Intermediate exam.

Performing Arts: The undergraduate degree in Performing Arts is a Bachelor of Arts (B.A.) Degree with specialisation in vocal/instrumental music/classical dance/drama. These courses are of 3-year duration and usually conducted in Gurukul Pattern. The Gurukul pattern is the ancient Indian pattern of education where all students (Shishya) used to live together as equals, irrespective of their social standing in the school (ashram) of the teacher (Guru) and learn from him.

The main objectives of the Performing Arts courses are:

- To provide professional training in the performing arts by keeping the creative atmosphere
- To build respect and understanding about the Indian performing arts cultural tradition.

---

[120] http://doa.org.in

Eligibility:

The eligibility required for Bachelor's Degree is a 12ᵗʰ standard pass, generally with minimum 45 to 50% marks depending on the university/institute offering it. Almost all institutes conduct an Entrance Test and an Interview. Usually, the course duration for this course is 3-4 years in most of the institutes and universities. Foundation and specialisation course are taught in the first and remaining years respectively.

One needs to really enjoy creating and imagining; this is one discipline where learning from others plays an important role in the growing process. One should know how to be radical in their ideas but be practical enough to create original, inspiring work.

List of Institutes offering Fine Art and Performing Art Bachelors Courses:

Table 29.1

#	Institute	Course	Subject	Entrance Test
		Fine Art		
1	Sir J.J.School of Art, Mumbai	4-year BFA	Painting, Textile Design, Interior Decoration, Sculpture, Metal Work, Ceramics, Applied Art	

#	Institute	Course	Subject	Entrance Test
2	Government School Of Art, Nagpur	4-year BFA	Painting, Textile Design, Applied Art	MH-AAC-CET
3	Government School of Art, Aurangabad	4-year BFA	Painting, Textile Design, Applied Art	
4	Rachana Sansad College of Applied Art and Craft, Mumbai	4-year BFA	Applied Art	
5	B. S. Bandekar College of Fine Art, (Applied Art) Sawantwadi	4-year BFA	Applied Art	
6	Padmashree D. Y. Patil College of Applied Art and Craft, Pune	4-year BFA	Applied Art	
7	Bharati Vidyapeeth's College of Fine Arts, Pune	4-year BFA	Applied Art	

8	Viva Institute of Applied Art, Shirgaon, Virar (E), Mumbai	4-year BFA	Applied Art	
9	Abhinav Kala Mahavidyalaya Pune	Diploma	1-year foundation + 4-year specialisation in Commercial or Fine Arts	SSC + Intermediate Drawing Exam
10	Chitralila Niketan, Pune	Diploma	1-year Foundation Diploma	SSC or HSC
11	L. S. Raheja School of Art	Diploma	1-year foundation + 4-year specialisation in Drawing and Painting or Applied Art	SSC + Intermediate Drawing Exam
Performing Art				
1	Lalit Kala Kendra (Centre for Performing Arts), University of Pune http://unipune.ac.in	3-year B.A.	Bachelor of Art in Music/Dance/Drama	12th pass + Entrance Test

2	School of Performing Arts, Bharati Vidyapeeth Deemed University, Pune	3-year B.A.	Bachelor of Art in Music/Dance	12th pass + Entrance Test

Career Prospects:

Arts graduates can work in various fields such as art studies, advertising companies, publishing houses, fashion houses etc. Many people are self-employed and are associated with product designers, manufacturers, publishing houses, software companies, magazines etc. Craftsmen also work as freelancers; they take part in exhibitions and host their own exhibitions where they find buyers for their creations.

They can also find employment in areas like animation, advertising companies, boutiques, dance studios, magazines, fashion houses, publishing houses, television, film and theatre direction/production/set design, textile industries. They can also work as Art Teachers in different institutes.

30

Bachelor of Vocation (B. Voc.)

The University Grants Commission (UGC)[121] has launched a scheme on skills development based higher education as part of college/university education, leading to Bachelor of Vocation (B.Voc.) under the NSQF (National Skills Qualifications Framework) under the Ministry of Human Resource Development. NSQF is a competency-based framework that organises all qualifications according to a series of levels of knowledge, skills and aptitude.

> The more we give importance to skill development, the more competent will be our youth...
>
> -Narendra Modi

The B.Voc. Programme is focused on universities and colleges providing undergraduate studies, which would also incorporate specific job roles with broad based general education. The main goal of the programme is to provide judicious mix of skills relating to a profession and appropriate content of general education and make the students job-ready

---

[121] http://www.ugc.ac.in

Objectives of the B.Voc. Programme:

- To provide judicious mix of skills relating to a profession and appropriate content of General Education.
- To ensure that the students have adequate knowledge and skills, so that they are work ready at each exit point of the programme.
- To provide flexibility to the students by means of pre-defined entry and multiple exit points.
- To enhance employability of the graduates and meet industry requirements.
- To provide vertical mobility to students completing 12th standard with vocational subjects.

Table 30.1 explains the different exit points and the type of certificates awarded after completing the levels.

Table 30.1

Level	Certificate awarded	Duration
First	Diploma	Completion of 1 year of vocational education after 12th standard
Second	Advanced Diploma	Completion of 2 years of vocational education after 12th standard
Third	Degree – B. Voc.	Completion of 3 years of vocational education after 12th standard

Eligibility: 12th standard or equivalent

Table 30.2

Networking and System Administration	Software Development
Jewellery Design and Gemmology	Multimedia and Animation
Software Development, Food Processing and Engineering	Retail Management
Industrial Automation	Automobile
Media and Communication	Digital Art and Animation
Tourism and Hospitality Management	Printing and Publishing
Building Technology	Agriculture
Interior Design	Soil and Water Conservation
Fashion Technology	Green House Technology
Food Processing Technology	Food Science Technology

Institutes offering B. Voc. Courses in Pune and Mumbai:

Table 30.3

1	University of Pune	Renewable Energy Jewellery Design and Gemmology
2	Ferguson College, Pune	Media and Communication Digital Art and Animation
3	PES Modern College of Arts, Pune	Green House Technology Food Processing Technology
4	PDEA Baburaoji Gholap College of Arts, Science and Commerce, Pune	Software Development Fashion Technology

5	Prof. Ramakrishna More Arts, Commerce and Science College, Pune	Software Development Food Science Technology
6	H.R. College of Commerce and Economics, Mumbai	Retail Management Tourism and Hospitality Management
7	Nagindas Khandwala College of Commerce Arts and Management Studies and Science, Mumbai	Retail Management Tourism and Hospitality Management
8	R.J. College of Arts, Science and Commerce, Mumbai	Real Estate Management Financial Markets and Services
9	Rajnarain Ruia College, Mumbai	Green House Management Travel and Tourism Management
10	St. Xavier's College, Mumbai	Software Development Tourism

31
Overseas Undergraduate Education

The trend of going overseas for higher education has been there in India since the last 40 years. Now a day, there is a noticeable rise in the number of students going abroad for their undergraduate studies as well, right after they complete their H.S.C. exam.

The most sought-after careers belong to the so-called STEM-related fields, viz. Science, Technology, Engineering, and Mathematics. The new areas that are gaining preference are Hospitality, Tourism, Psychology, Geology, Management, and Design.

The most popular countries for undergraduate education are the United States of America and the United Kingdom. Germany, Australia, Canada, and Singapore have also started gaining consideration.

Salient features of overseas education:

A. Quality of Education:

- The educational environment is quite different than that in India. The focus is on self-learning than rote learning. The student has control on what to learn and how to learn.
- Multifaceted curricula, assessments and teaching methods.
- Extensive use of technology in education.

- Easy accessibility of faculty and encouragement and support for conducting research.
- Flexibility – most of the overseas universities and colleges offer flexible curricula, where a student can choose inter-disciplinary subjects as the majors and minors. One is also given an opportunity to change a major if he/she wishes to.

B. Personality Development:

- Students become more independent and self-reliant.
- Develop self-learning abilities and research aptitude.
- Widen horizons because of the exposure to the culturally diverse population and exchange of ideas amongst the peers.

C. Global job opportunities: -

- Due to the global exposure during education, there is a high probability that one may get a global career / job opportunity. -

Education in USA:

There are more than 4500 accredited institutions offering different types of course in USA. The institutions in USA are accredited by independent accrediting bodies rather than by a national or regional level accreditation body. The different types of institutions in USA are:

Liberal Arts Institutions: Offering courses in the arts, humanities, languages, and social and physical sciences. Majority of them are private institutions and hence most of them are usually smaller than the public institutions.

Community Colleges: These colleges provide two-year associate degree programs, which prepare students to continue studies for an undergraduate degree or occupational skill enhancement.

State Colleges and Universities (Public Universities): They are subsidised by U.S. State governments and generally are very large in size.

USA has world's most flexible educational system where students are allowed to select subjects, which they are interested in. The education system in USA is a credit-based system in which the students earn credits for courses they complete; these earned credits count towards the completion of a program. Usually a student selects one major subject with some minor courses. Courses are often divided into "core" subject areas to provide the foundation of the degree program and "major" courses to provide specialisation in a subject area. Students can also take "elective" courses to explore other topics of interest for a well-rounded educational experience.

The U.S. academic calendar typically runs from September to May and can be divided into two academic terms of 16-18 weeks known as semesters. Alternatively, some schools may operate on a quarter or trimester system of multiple terms of 10-12 weeks.

A typical undergraduate bachelor's degree in USA is a 4-year degree: Bachelor of Arts (BA or AB), Bachelor of Science (BS), Bachelor of Fine Arts (BFA), Bachelor or Engineering degree (B. Engg.), Bachelor of Architecture (B.Arch.).

Medicine, Dentistry, Law courses are offered after completing the 4-year undergraduate degree (B.A. / B.S.)

through a common entrance test appropriate to the respective field.

Admission Process:

The U.S. does not have a centralised admissions process and a student can apply to as many institutes as he/she wants. Some institutes use Common Application[122] or Universal College Application[123] services. A student can apply to a number of institutes which are a member of either of this service. The advantage for the student is that student doesn't need to apply with a single application to the member institutes. The essay question and personal details can be submitted only once for all selected member institutes which substantially saves a student's time. It's a good thing because it gives you more liberty and freedom in choosing which schools to apply to, but it also means much more work on your part, because you then need to prepare different applications for different universities.

. If you are looking to study somewhere with a wider variety of opportunities, then the U.S. could be the right place for you. Not only do you get to meet people from all around the world, but you also can become a well-rounded person.

- Eligibility: H.S.C. certification from a recognised board in India (including IB Diploma)
- Application Requirements:
- Academic records (usually from 9 to 12 standard)

---

[122] https://www.commonapp.org
[123] https://www.universalcollegeapp.com

- Standardised Tests: Scholastic Aptitude Test (SAT)[124] or American College Testing (ACT)[125] test. Some universities also ask for SAT subject tests.
- English Proficiency Tests (for International Students): Test of English as a Foreign Language (TOEFL)[126], International English Language Testing System (IELTS)[127] or Pearson Tests of English (PTE)[128]
- Letters of Recommendation: Generally two letters of recommendation are required. Out of these, one has to be sent from the School Counselor and second can be from a subject teacher.

A letter of recommendation (also called reference letter), is a document in which the writer (teacher/school counselor) assesses the qualities, characteristics, and capabilities of the person (student) being recommended in terms of that student's ability to perform in academics, extracurricular activities, team activities etc.

- College Essay: Generally for the undergraduate admissions, the student needs to submit an Essay for which some prompts are given. The applicant has to choose one prompt (Essay topic) and write an essay. Generally the word limit is about 600 - 700 words.
- Personal Statement or Resume: Some universities also ask for a Personal Statement, Resume or an additional essay.

---

[124] https://collegereadiness.collegeboard.org/sat
[125] http://www.act.org
[126] http://www.ets.org/toefl
[127] https://www.ielts.org
[128] http://pearsonpte.com/

- o A personal statement is a written account which describes the applicant as a person, his/her family background, goals in life, hobbies and skills etc.
- Other documents: Other documents may include:
  - o Financial Statement
  - o Passport Copy
  - o Portfolio (for students applying for Design, Fine Art or Architecture programmes). A **portfolio** is a compilation of materials that demonstrates a student's skills, knowledge, education, training, and experiences.
- Audition: Students applying for Performing Arts may be called in for auditions.
- Interview: Some institutes, especially Art and Design related institutes, may require an Interview. The interview is usually conducted through a Skype call, or Face Time audio or video call.

Education in UK:

The UK has a well-deserved reputation worldwide for providing high quality and well-respected higher education. There are 160 universities and colleges in the UK that award an undergraduate bachelor's degree. The bachelor's with honours degree in UK is of 3-year duration. Examples of Bachelor's degrees in UK are: Bachelor of Arts (B.A.), Bachelor of Education (B.Ed.), Bachelor of Law (L.L.B.), Bachelor of Science (B.Sc.), Bachelor of Engineering (B.Engg.), Bachelor of Medicine (M.B.).

Some institutions in UK have degree awarding powers and are recognised by the UK authorities (UK and Scottish Parliament, Welsh and Northern Ireland Assemblies).

There are also several hundred colleges and other institutions which do not have degree-awarding powers but who provide complete courses leading to recognised UK degrees. Courses at these institutions are validated by institutions which have degree awarding powers.

Admission Process:

A. The Universities and Colleges Admissions Service (UCAS)[129] is a UK-based organisation, which operates the undergraduate application process.

B. Eligibility: H.S.C. certification from a recognised board in India (including IB Diploma)

C. Application Requirements:

D. Academic records (usually from 9 to 12 standard)

E. English Proficiency Tests (for International Students): International English Language Testing System (IELTS) or Pearson Tests of English (PTE), Test of English as a Foreign Language (TOEFL) - Preferably IELTS

F. Personal Statement: One should explain why he/she wants to study in UK, goals in life etc.

G. Other documents: Other documents may include Financial Statement, Passport Copy, Portfolio (For students applying for Design, Fine Art or Architecture programmes). An audition may be required for students applying for Performing Arts.

H. Interview: Some institutes, especially Art and Design may require an Interview. The interview is usually

---

[129] https://www.ucas.com

conducted through a Skype call or FaceTime audio or video call.

Australia and New Zealand:

Bachelor's degree in Australia and New Zealand is conferred after 3 to 4 years, depending on the course. In addition to the application and transcripts, IELTS is the only pre-requisite to apply to colleges in Australia and New Zealand. They don't generally ask for standardized test scores. The academic year starts in February, ends in November and generally consists of two semesters. Marine Biology, Marine Engineering, Environmental Studies, Veterinary Science, along with the regular Management and Engineering courses, are the most sought after courses in these two countries.

Singapore:

The strength of Singapore's education system lies in its broad-based curriculum where innovation and entrepreneurship are the priority. The Ministry of Education in Singapore controls and directs the education policy in Singapore. There are Government funded Polytechnics and Universities in Singapore. The National University of Singapore (NUS) is a world famous university. The most sought after programs are Business Management, Accountancy, Economics, Information Systems management, Law and Social Sciences.

Admissions to Singapore universities are highly competitive. One needs to apply to all universities separately. The application material required are transcripts, English Proficiency and SAT scores.

Applying to the Overseas Institutions:

- Overseas admission is a 'Project' by itself. One needs to plan ahead for it. Once you have decided to study overseas, start your research in the following areas:

  o Decide the Major / Honours in which you would like to pursue your career
  o Decide the country in which you would like to study. Some of the main deciding factors would be - quality of education of the chosen major in that country, cost of education (cost of education + living cost), course duration

- Research about the admission process in that country:
  o Whether it is a centralised admission process
  o When does the academic year start
  o What are the application requirements
  o What is the application deadline: The deadlines change as per the country. For e.g. in USA the regular deadlines are usually between mid-January till 1ˢᵗ February, while that in Australia are in late October to November for the term commencing in February of the subsequent year
  o Whether any standardised tests are required for admission (For e.g. SAT score is required for undergraduate admission in USA and in Singapore as well)
  o Which English Proficiency Test is required (For e.g. TOEFL is required in USA, IELTS is required in UK, Australia, Canada, IELTS is also accepted in Singapore and in many US institutes)

- o What are the writing samples required - such as Essays (USA), Statement of Purpose (UK, Australia, New Zealand) are required to be submitted along with the application.
- o Some tips for writing an essay / SOP - Write about - Who you are, who you want to be and how this education will you to achieve your goal. And most importantly - Be Creative, Think Futuristic and Think Unique!
- o Recommendation letters (school counselors, academic teachers)
- o Proof of financial support - whether it is required at the time of application or later after receiving the confirmation of admission

- Start preparing for the entrance exam - Similar to India, the overseas undergraduate admissions are highly competitive hence getting a good test score is of utmost importance. The SAT exam is valid for five years hence it will be a good idea to prepare for SAT right in the beginning of 11th standard and appear for SAT in November or December in the same year. This serves two purposes - (i) If the scores are not good you can repeat the test and/or prepare for SAT subject test (SAT 2) and (ii) You have ample time to focus on your studies as grades are also a very important factor which is considered in the selection process. More information about SAT is available on the College Board[130] website, which is an American private non-profit corporation that develops and administers SAT.

---

[130] https://www.collegeboard.org

- English Proficiency (TOEFL / IELTS) - These tests are comparatively easy than SAT, you can appear as per your convenience.
- Shortlisting the schools: On the basis of your research about the schools is complete then shortlist a number of schools where you would like to study.
- Check the expiry date of your passport
- Find out about the types of accommodations available
- Find out more information about the region where you are going to study.

32

Information about some emerging fields

This chapter gives information about some of the newer upcoming fields. Please note these careers start after a basic undergraduate degree in a related field. One may then decide to take a master's course, a post-graduate diploma or a certificate course according to the requirement of that field. For e.g. a career in bioinformatics can start with an undergraduate degree in computer science or biotechnology supported with courses in computer science.

Bioinformatics

Bioinformatics is an interdisciplinary field that develops methods and software tools for understanding biological data. It combines computer science, statistics, mathematics and engineering to analyse and interpret biological data.

Bioinformatics has become an important part of many areas of biology where it helps in extraction of useful results from large amounts of raw data. In the filed of genetics and genomics, it helps in sequencing and annotating genomes and their observed mutations. It also plays a role in the analysis of gene and protein expression and regulations. It also aids in the simulation and modeling of DNA, RNA and protein structures as well as molecular interactions.

Bioinformatics specialists are computer and data specialists who work within biotechnology and other biological research areas. They collect, store, analyse and present complex biological data that can include DNA and genome information, protein sequencing and pathways. The day-to-day duties of bioinformatics specialists can include:

- Designing and manipulating complex databases
- Creating web-based analytical tools and algorithms
- Developing new software for project and research needs

Nanotechnology:

Nano science and nanotechnology are the study and application of extremely small things (about 1 to 100 nanometers in size) and can be used across all the other science fields, such as chemistry, biology, physics, materials science, and engineering.

Nanotechnology is helping scientists make our homes, cars, and businesses more energy-efficient through new fuel cells, batteries, and solar panels. It is also helping to find ways to purify drinking water and to detect and clean up environmental waste and damage.

Applications of Nanotechnology/Nano materials:
Nanotechnology and Nano materials are used in various areas such as –

- Nanoscale additives are used in polymer composite materials for tennis rackets, motorcycle helmets, automobile bumpers, luggage etc. to make them light weight, stiff, durable and resilient.

- Nanoscale thin films on eyeglasses, computer and camera displays, windows, and other surfaces
- Nanoscale materials in cosmetic products provide greater clarity or coverage; cleansing; absorption; etc.
- Nano-engineered materials are used to make food containers to minimise carbon dioxide leakage or reduce oxygen inflow, moisture outflow, or the growth of bacteria
- Nano technologically produced polymer material is used in food and beverage containers, fuel storage tanks for aircraft and automobiles, in aerospace components because of its thermal, mechanical and barrier properties.
- Nano-engineered materials are used in automotive products such as high-power rechargeable battery systems; lower-rolling-resistance tires; high-efficiency/low-cost sensors and electronics or in household products such as stain removers, air purifiers and filters, specialised paints and sealing products.
- Nano-structured ceramic coatings exhibit much greater toughness than conventional wear-resistant coatings for machine parts.
- Nanoparticles are used increasingly in catalysis to boost chemical reactions.
- In healthcare, nano-ceramics are used in some dental implants or to fill holes in diseased bones. Opticians apply nano-coatings to eyeglasses to make them easier to keep clean and harder to scratch.
- Nanotechnology helps build new transistor structures and interconnects for the fastest, most advanced computing chips.

- Nanotechnology-based medicines are now in clinical trials, which may be available soon to treat patients. Some use nanoparticles to deliver toxic anti-cancer drugs targeted directly to tumours, minimising drug damage to other parts of the body. Others help medical imaging tools, like MRIs and CAT scans, work better and more safely.

Aerospace Technology:

Aerospace technology is a field that deals with the technical side of aerospace missions. Aerospace technologists are professionals who work independently or as part of a team. They conduct research, and design and develop vehicles and systems for atmospheric and space environments. One can work in this field as a scientist or as an engineer. Careers path can begin at a graduate level with Physics, Mathematics, Life Sciences or with an Engineering degree in Aerospace or related field such as Mechanical. Other undergraduate degrees that may also lead to this career path can be Chemistry, Geology, Meteorology, etc.

Some Kinds of Aerospace Careers are:

- Astronaut, Mission Specialist, Pilot Astronaut
- Scientists - Astronomy, Chemistry, Geology, Meteorology, Oceanography, Physics, Life Sciences (Medical doctor, Psychologist, Biologist, Nutritionist, Physiologist), Computer Science, Statistics, Mathematics
- Systems Analyst
- Engineers - Aerospace, Biomedical, Chemical, Computer, Civil, Mechanical, Industrial, Petrochemical etc.

245

- Architectural designers

Actuarial Science:

Actuarial science is the discipline that applies mathematical and statistical methods to assess risk in insurance, finance and other industries and professions. The responsibilities of actuarial scientists include designing and pricing of policies, monitoring the adequacy of the funds to provide the promised benefits, recommending fair rate of bonus where applicable, valuation of the insurance business, ensuring solvency margin and other insurance risks like legal liability, loss of profit, etc. They also define the risk factors, advise on the premia to be charged and re-insurance to be purchased, calculate reserve for outstanding claims and carry out financial modeling.[131]

A career in Actuarial Science may start with an undergraduate degree in Mathematics, Statistics, Computer Science, and Economics or with a CA, CMA or CS qualification.

Intellectual Property:

Intellectual property refers to creations of the mind: inventions; literary and artistic works; and symbols, names and images used in commerce. Intellectual property rights are mechanism to grant exclusive right of certain creative ideas or business concepts to any individual or business entity. Intellectual property is divided into two categories:

---

[131] http://www.actuariesindia.org

i. **Industrial Property:** includes patents for inventions, trademarks, industrial designs and geographical indications.

ii. **Copyright covers:** literary works (such as novels, poems and plays), films, music, artistic works (e.g., drawings, paintings, photographs and sculptures) and architectural design. Rights related to copyright include those of performing artists in their performances, producers of phonograms in their recordings, and broadcasters in their radio and television program

Protection of intellectual property has become so important that companies today carry out intellectual property audits to identify their intellectual wealth and form special departments to manage them. Presently, almost every country is taking measures to strengthen its shield against cases related to intellectual property. India also has formulated specific laws on a variety of aspects related to intellectual property.

Patent: A patent is an exclusive right granted for an invention –a product or process that provides a new way of doing something, or that offers a new technical solution to a problem. A patent provides patent owners with protection for their inventions. Protection is granted for a limited period, generally 20 years.

Patents provide incentives to individuals by recognising their creativity and offering the possibility of material reward for their marketable inventions. These incentives encourage innovation, which in turn enhances the quality of human life

Trademark: A trademark is a distinctive sign that identifies certain goods or services produced or provided by an individual or a company. Its origin dates back to ancient times when craftsmen reproduced their signatures, or "marks", on their artistic works or products of a functional or practical nature. The "tick-mark" sign on Nike, one of the global mega-giant manufacturer of sports-goods is known to all of us.

A career in **Intellectual Property Rights** (IPR), Patenting and Trademark is one of the upcoming careers. Engineers, Scientists also have a future in this field and can work as Patent inspector. Graduate from any faculty can become a Trade Mark Agent after clearing the Trade Mark Agent Exam. Law Graduates can directly become Trade Mark Agents without appearing for any other additional examination. More information can be found on the website of Controller General of Patents Designs and Trademarks[132]. The National Law Universities in India offer different post graduate diploma and degree courses Intellectual Property Rights as well as other special areas of law.

---

[132] http://www.ipindia.nic.in

33
End Notes

In this book, the term 'Career' is used multiple times. Let us now understand how the term is used multiple contexts.

Career is defined by the Oxford English Dictionary as a person's "course or progress through life (or a distinct portion of life)". Hence, in this definition, career relates to a range of aspects of an individual's life, learning and work.

Another context in which the term career is used, is to describe an occupation or a profession that usually involves special training or formal education which is considered as a person's work area in his/her life. In this case, a career is seen as what the person aspires to be in future, what kind of work s/he prefers to do; for e.g., a career in computer science, a career in designing, a career in health science, a career in management or finance etc.

"Career Development" is a process of planning and managing one's education, work and related aspects towards shaping the aspired career. For e.g. a student aspiring to be an Ophthalmologist (Eye Surgeon), would choose a science stream in 11th and 12th standard, then prepare for the Medical Entrance Examination, get admission in a Medical College, complete MBBS then appear for the Postgraduate entrance test to get admission in the Post graduate course in Ophthalmology specialty and become an Ophthalmologist. S/he will then decide to start an independent practice or work in a hospital.

Thus we say that this person has achieved what s/he aspired to be. But still to make a successful career as an Ophthalmologist, s/he has to continuously keep his/her knowledge and skills updated. Hence while practicing as an Ophthalmologist, he/she might think of gaining more advanced skills by doing some Fellowships, attending conferences, workshops. Hence, the process of "Career Development" is a continuous process and it depends on individuals, themselves how they want to **shape their career**. It requires meticulous planning and management.

Sometimes, due to some reasons, a plan may not work out, for e.g. not able to score good score in the entrance test, not

> A Plan-B life can be just as good or better than Plan-A life. You just have to let go of that first dream and realize that God has already written the first chapter of the new life that awaits you. All you have to do is start reading!
>
> -Shannon A. Alder (Inspirational Author)

becoming eligible for a certain course. Don't get disheartened because if you keep on thinking about the past, you won't be able to think of the future. The knowledge you gain will always equip you, and even though Plan A didn't work out, there always be a Plan B.

The Planning Process:

- **Think about your interests, abilities, competency and skills** - Which subjects you like the most and you score well. This will help you to choose an appropriate stream. An aptitude test report will give you guidance in understanding your abilities and skills.

- **Explore choices and take an informed decision** - Find out more about the subjects in different streams in the 11th and 12th standard. What are you supposed to learn, how scoring the subject is, is it somewhat related to what i learned up to 10th standard or totally different etc. While you are doing this, constantly introspect and judge yourself.

- Before taking the decision, once again, ask questions to yourself - Do I have the **interest**? Do I have the **ability**? and Am I **competent** for it?

- **Research** (aspired career/s) - Find out more about the careers you have in mind. For e.g. if you are interested in hospitality management then what skills are required in this field, do I have the required skills, if not, what can I do to enhance these skills. It would be a great idea to talk to people already in this field, the alumni and current students of a college.

- **Research** (different pathways) - Once you decide a career, research about the different pathways that lead to it. For example - a career as a computer scientist can begin from a bachelor's degree in computer science or with an engineering degree in computer science. Here it is of utmost important to find out about the subjects in both the areas, their difficulty levels, duration of the course and then take a decision.

- **Research** (Eligibility Requirement) - Once you have decided what to do, find out how to get there, find out about the eligibility criteria, entrance tests etc. For e.g. For B.Sc. Computer there is the admission process is not centralised thus there is no common entrance test. But the student needs to apply to every college separately and each college might conduct their own entrance test. Similarly, for design courses, the student needs to show a portfolio of work, which one needs to prepare well in advance. If there is an entrance test, find out the month in which it is usually conducted, when are the forms made available, when is the last date of application etc.

- **Research** (Accreditation) - When you select an institution do check its accreditation / affiliation. Some of the factors you need to check are:

  o Whether the course is recognised by the University Grants Commission, check for NAAC Accreditation (National Assessment and Accreditation Council)

  o Whether the course and institute requires an approval from a regulatory body, for e.g. the engineering, architecture, pharmacy, hotel management, MBA colleges need to be approved by AICTE (All India Council for Technical Education. Medical colleges require an approval from Medical Council of India[133], the architecture course needs to be approved by Council of Architecture etc.

  o In addition, all engineering, architecture, hotel management, pharmacy, MCA, MBA courses in Maharashtra State require an approval from the Directorate of Technical Education (DTE). The DTE website provides detailed information about the institutes recognised by them, including courses offered, number of seats, available facilities etc.

---

[133] http://www.mciindia.org

- o Find out more information about the institution you want to join - search the internet, talk to alumni, current students, if possible see the books.

- o Sometimes this whole exercise may still prove to be inadequate. A career advisor, who is an expert and is well informed in this field, may be of help in such a case. A career advisor is a person who can help you plan a career relevant to your education and aptitude.

> Education is our passport to the future, for tomorrow belongs to the people who prepare for it today...
>
> -Malcolm X. (Human Rights Activist)

Preparing for the future may seem intimidating and overwhelming, through research and planning would take you to the path of success. Here are some tips to achieve that:

Goal Setting:

- Focus on what you want to do in the future. Write down what you want to do.
- Think about the steps you will take to achieve this.
- It should be a SMART Goal (Specific, Measurable, Achievable, Realistic and Time-based). For e.g. I will maintain my 10th standard marks in 11th standard is a SMART goal as it is Specific, can be measured, achievable, realistic because you have not set very high expectations for yourself and obviously time-based)
- Set short-term goals, because (i) They are easy to achieve (ii) goals may change over time hence it is easier to set another short term goal

- It will be a good idea to stick this paper in such a place from where you will easily read it every day (a wardrobe door might be an idea place). This helps in a big way to keep one motivated.

> There is one quality which one must possess to win, and that is definiteness of purpose...
>
> the knowledge of what one wants, and a burning desire to possess it.

Time Management:

- You might have many classes at different places in addition to the colleges classes. Organising your routine is a big task. It does not only include time management but also includes organising the required books, transport, food etc.

Study Habits:

- Appropriate note taking, highlighting and organisation of topics to study will enhance your learning. If you have any queries regarding a topic, don't hesitate to ask a teacher.

Clear Communication:

- Talk openly with your parents about your aspirations, seek their advise, if you feel your opinions differ, then find out the reason and if you are convicted that you don't want to pursue a career suggested by them tell them why you feel so in an assertive way.

Skill Building:

- Once you are admitted in a course of your choice, learn about appropriate additional skills required for that particular field. For e.g. improving public speaking or presentation skills during the undergraduate course or doing an internship during summer vacation etc.

And last but not the least, do remember, your flight is just taking off and yet to fly in the stratosphere!! Be focused, and set goal and remain motivated to achieve them. That is the real path to career success!

> He who would learn to fly, one day must learn to stand and walk and run and climb and dance; one cannot fly into flying.
>
> -Friedrich Nietzsche (German Philosopher & Poet)

Important entrance tests after 12th standard examination:

AIPMT	All India Medical and Dental	May
BIT-SAT	Birla Institute of Technology - Engineering Science, Pharmacy	May
CLAT	Common Law Entrance - All India	May
CPT	CA-Common Proficiency Test	June & Dec
CS Foundation	Company Secretary Foundation Course	June & Dec
CWA Foundation	Eligibility for Cost Accountancy Foundation Course	June & Dec
FEAT*	FLAME University, Pune - ALL UG courses including Liberal Arts	Once in Jan, Feb, Mar., Apr.
IBB (Pune Univ.)	Institute of Bioinformatics & Biotechnology	June/July

IISER	Pure Science (Physics, Math, Chemistry, Biology)	June/July
JEE Advance	IIT, IISER	May
JEE Main	Engineering, IIIT, Architecture	April
MAH-HM-CET	Maharashtra State Hotel Management	May
MH-AAC-CET	Maharashtra State Fine Art CET	May
MH-CET	Maharashtra State - Engineering, Pharmacy, Health Sciences	May
MH-Law CET	Maharashtra State Law Entrance Test	May
MITID-DAT	MIT Institute of Design, Pune	April
NATA	Architecture Eligibility	April to May & June to August
NCHMJEE	All India Hotel Management	April
NEED	National Institute of Design, Ahmedabad	January
NIFT	National Institute of Fashion Technology, New Delhi	February
Phase-2 Entrance	DSK International School (Phase I-Document review, Phase II - Aptitude Test)	March
SAT	Once in a month, EXCEPT in the month of February, April and from July to September	
SEAT	Srishti Institute of Art, Design & Technology	April
SET*	Symbiosis Entrance Test for - ALL UG courses from Symbiosis	May

	University including Liberal Arts, Economics, Law	
UCEED	Indian Institute of Information Technology, Design & Manufacturing, IIT Mumbai	January

FLAME and Symbiosis University also accept SAT scores

Useful Links:

1	A.F.M.C., Pune	http://www.afmc.nic.in
2	All India Council for Technical Education (A.I.C.T.E.)	http://www.aicte-india.org
3	All India Institute of Medical Sciences (AIIMS)	http://www.aiims.edu/en.html
4	All India Pre-Medical / Pre-Dental Test (AIPMT)	http://aipmt.nic.in
5	Alliance Français	http://www.afindia.org
6	American College Testing (ACT)	http://www.act.org
7	Apprenticeship Training	http://www.apprentice-engineer.com
8	Ashoka University	http://www.ashoka.edu.in
9	Association of Indian Universities (AIU)	http://www.aiu.ac.in
10	Association of Managements of Unaided Private Medical & Dental Colleges (AMUPMDC)	http://www.amupmdc.org
11	Bar Council of India	http://barcouncilofindia.org
12	Birla Institute of Technology (BITS)	http://www.bits-pilani.ac.in

13	Birla Institute of Technology (BITS) at Mesra, Ranchi	https://www.bitmesra.ac.in
14	Central Board of Secondary Education (C.B.S.E.)	http://cbse.nic.in
15	Centre for Development of Advanced Computing (CDAC)	http://www.cdac.in
16	Centre for Excellence in Basic Sciences (CBS)	http://www.cbs.ac.in
17	Chennai Mathematics Institute	http://www.cmi.ac.in
18	Christ University, Bengaluru	http://www.christuniversity.in/economics/programmes
19	Christian Medical College, Ludhiana (CMC-Ludhiana)	http://cmcludhiana.in
20	Christian Medical College, Vellore (CMC-Vellore)	http://www.cmch-vellore.edu
21	College Board	https://www.collegeboard.org
22	Combined Defence Services Examination	http://www.upsc.gov.in/general/cds.htm
23	Common Application	https://www.commonapp.org
24	Controller General of Patents Designs and Trademarks	http://www.ipindia.nic.in
25	Council for the Indian School Certificate Exam (I.C.S.E.)	http://www.cisce.org
26	Council of Architecture	http://www.coa.gov.in
27	D.Y. Patil International College, Lohegaon	http://www.internationalcollege.in
28	Department of Atomic Energy (DAE)	http://dae.nic.in

29	Department of Foreign Languages, University of Pune	http://www.unipune.ac.in/dept/fine_arts/foreign_languages
30	Dhirubhai Ambani Institute of Information and Communication Technology	http://www.daiict.ac.in
31	Directorate General of Civil Aviation (DGCA)	http://dgca.nic.in
32	Directorate General of Shipping (DG Shipping)	http://dgshipping.gov.in
33	Directorate of Medical Education & Research (DMER)	http://www.dmer.org
34	Directorate of Technical Education (DTE Maharashtra)	http://www.dtemaharashtra.gov.in
35	Directorate of Vocational Education & Training (DVET)	http://www.dvet.gov.in
36	DOA, Maharashtra State	http://doa.org.in
37	DSK International School of Design	http://dskic.in
38	Fergusson College, Pune	http://www.fergusson.edu
39	FLAME University	http://www.flame.edu.in
40	Goethe-Institut - Max Mueller Bhavan	http://www.goethe.de
41	IDC, IIT Bombay	http://www.iitb.ac.in/uceed/2016
42	IELTS	https://www.ielts.org
43	IISER Bhopal	https://www.iiserbhopal.ac.in
44	IISER Kolkata	http://www.iiserkol.ac.in
45	IISER Mohali	http://www.iisermohali.ac.in
46	IISER Pune	http://www.iiserpune.ac.in

47	IISER Thiruvananthapuram	http://www.iisertvm.ac.in
48	IISER Tirupati	http://www.iisertirupati.ac.in
49	IIT Banaras Hindu University	http://www.iitbhu.ac.in
50	IIT Bombay	http://www.iitb.ac.in
51	IIT Delhi	http://www.iitd.ac.in
52	IIT Guwahati	http://www.iitg.ac.in
53	IIT Kharagpur	http://www.iitkgp.ac.in
54	IIT Madras	https://biotech.iitm.ac.in/
55	IIT Roorke	http://www.iitr.ac.in
56	IIT Roorki	http://www.iitr.ac.in/departments/BT
57	Indian Air Force	http://careerairforce.nic.in
58	Indian Coast Guard	http://www.joinindiancoastguard.gov.in/officerentry.html
59	Indian Council of Agricultural Research (ICAR)	http://icarexam.net
60	Indian Institute of Information Technology (IIIT), Allahabad	http://www.iiita.ac.in/
61	Indian Institute of Information Technology and Management, Gwalior	http://www.iiitm.ac.in
62	Indian Institute of Information Technology, Design & Manufacturing, Jabalpur (IITDM)	http://design.iiitdmj.ac.in
63	Indian Institute of Information Technology, Design and Manufacturing (IIITDM), Chennai	http://www.iiitdm.ac.in/
64	Indian Institute of Science (IISc)	http://www.iisc.ernet.in

65	Indian Institute of Tourism and Travel Management	www.iittm.net
66	Indian Maritime University (IMU)	http://www.imu.edu.in/
67	Indian School of Design & Education in collaboration with Parsons, New York	http://www.isdi.in
68	Indian Statistical Institute at Kolkata, Delhi, Bangalore, Chennai & Tezpur	http://www.isical.ac.in
69	Indira Gandhi National Open University (IGNOU)	http://www.ignou.ac.in
70	Indira Gandhi Rashtriya Uran Akademi (IGRUA)	http://igrua.gov.in
71	Indus International School, Bhukum	http://www.indusschoolpune.com
72	Institute of Bioinformatics & Biotechnology, Pune University	http://www.unipune.ac.in/snc/institut e_of_bioinformatics_and_biotechnolo gy/
73	Institute of Chartered Accountants of India (ICAI)	http://www.icai.org
74	Institute of Company Secretaries of India (ICSI)	http://www.icsi.edu
75	Institute of Cost Accountants of India	http://icmai.in
76	Instituto Hispania	http://www.institutohispania.com
77	International Baccalaureate (IB)	http://www.ibo.org
78	International School Aamby, Lonavala	http://www.internationalschoolaamby. com

79	Jawaharlal Institute of Postgraduate Medical Education & Research (JIPMER)	http://jipmer.edu.in/
80	Jawaharlal Nehru University, New Delhi (JNU)	http://www.jnu.ac.in
81	JEE Main	http://jeemain.nic.in
82	Join Indian Army	http://www.joinindianarmy.nic.in/
83	Join Indian Navy	http://www.joinindiannavy.gov.in
84	MAEER's MIT Institute of Design, Pune	http://www.mitid.edu.in
85	Maharashtra Animal & Fishery Sciences University (MAFSU)	http://www.mafsu.in
86	Maharashtra Council for Agriculture Education & Research (MCAER)	http://www.mcaer.org/
87	Maharashtra State Board of Secondary & Higher Secondary Education (MSBSHSE)	https://mahahsscboard.maharashtra.gov.in
88	Maharashtra State Board of Technical Education (MSBTE)	http://www.msbte.com/
89	Maharashtra State Council of Education Research and Training	http://www.mscert.org.in
90	Maharashtra University of Health Sciences (MUHS)	http://www.muhs.ac.in
91	Mahatma Gandhi Institute of Medical Sciences (MGIMS), Sewagram	https://www.mgims.ac.in
92	Malaviya National Institute of Technology, Jaipur	http://www.mnit.ac.in

93	Maulana Azad National Institute of Technology, Bhopal	http://www.manit.ac.in
94	Medical Council of India	http://www.mciindia.org/
95	Mercedes-Benz International School, Hinjewadi	http://mbis.org
96	MHRD-Centrally Funded Technical Institutes (CFTI)	http://mhrd.gov.in/technical-education-1
97	Ministry of Human Resource, IIIT (MHRD)	http://mhrd.gov.in/iiits
98	MSBSHSE - Aptitude Test Notification	http://www.sscboardpune.in/eng/wp-content/uploads/2016/01/SSC-SKILL-TEST-IMP.pdf
99	Mumbai University	http://mu.ac.in
100	National Aptitude Test in Architecture (NATA)	https://www.nata.in
101	National Council for Hotel Management & Catering Technology	http://www.nchm.nic.in
102	National Council for Teacher Education	http://ncte-india.org
103	National Institute of Design, Ahmedabad (NID)	http://www.nid.edu
104	National Institute of Fashion Technology, New Delhi (NIFT)	http://www.nift.ac.in
105	National Institute of Mental Health and Neurosciences (NIMHANS)	http://nimhans.ac.in
106	National Institute of Science Education & Research, Odisha (NISER)	http://www.niser.ac.in

107	National Institute of Technology, Calicut	http://www.nitc.ac.in
108	National Institute of Technology, Hamirpur	http://www.nith.ac.in
109	National Institute of Technology, Patna	http://www.nitp.ac.in
110	National Institute of Technology, Raipur	http://www.nitrr.ac.in
111	National Institute of Technology, Rourkela	http://nitrkl.ac.in
112	National Institute of Technology, Tiruchirappalli	http://www.nitt.edu
113	NISER's National Entrance Screening Test (NEST)	https://www.nestexam.in
114	Pandit Dwarka Prasad Mishra Indian Institute of Information Technology, Design and Manufacturing (IIITDM), Jabalpur	http://www.iiitdmj.ac.in
115	Pearson Tests of English (PTE)	http://pearsonpte.com/
116	S. N. D. T. College, Pune	http://sndthsc.com/
117	S. N. D. T. Women's University, Mumbai	http://sndt.ac.in
118	S.P.Jain School of Global Management	http://www.spjain.org/bec/index.aspx
119	Savitribai Phule Pune University (Pune University)	http://www.unipune.ac.in
120	Scholastic Aptitude Test (SAT)	https://collegereadiness.collegeboard.org/sat

121	School of Language & Literature, Jawaharlal Nehru University, New Delhi	http://www.jnu.ac.in/SLLCS
122	School of Planning & Architecture, Bhopal	http://www.spabhopal.ac.in
123	School of Planning & Architecture, New Delhi	http://www.spa.ac.in
124	School of Planning & Architecture, Vijayawada	http://www.spav.ac.in
125	Srishti School of Design, Bangalore	http://srishti.ac.in
126	Symbiosis Institute of Design	http://sid.edu.in
127	Symbiosis Institute of Foreign and Indian Languages (SIFIL)	http://www.sifil-symbiosis.org/courses.html
128	Symbiosis International School, Viman Nagar	http://symbiosisinternationalschool.net
129	Symbiosis School of Economics	http://sse.ac.in/
130	Symbiosis School of Liberal Arts	http://www.ssla.edu.in
131	Tata Institute of Social Sciences (TISS)	http://www.tiss.edu
132	TOEFL	http://www.ets.org/toefl
133	Topiwala National Medical College (TNMC), Mumbai	http://www.tnmcnair.com
134	Undergraduate Common Entrance Examination for Design (UCEED) IIT-Bombay	http://www.iitb.ac.in/uceed/2016/
135	Union Public Service Commission	http://www.upsc.gov.in
136	Universal College Application	https://www.universalcollegeapp.com

137	Universities and College Admissions Services (UCAS)	https://www.ucas.com
138	University Grants Commission	http://www.ugc.ac.in
139	University of Delhi (Business Economics)	http://www.du.ac.in/du/index.php?page=business-economics
140	UWC Mahindra College, Mulshi	http://uwcmahindracollege.org
141	Vellore Institute of Technology	http://vit.ac.in/
142	Veterinary Council of India (VCI)	http://www.vci.nic.in
143	Victorious Kidss Educares, Kharadi	http://www.victoriouskidsseducares.org
144	Visvesvaraya National Institute of Technology, Nagpur	http://vnit.ac.in

Profile of the Author

Savita Marathe
M.Sc. (Clinical) Embryology,
University of Leeds, UK
PGDHHM
Fellowship in Medical Education

- Savita is an educationist and an accomplished trainer and certified career advisor. She has extensive coaching experience in communication skills, education technology, curriculum development, instructional and workshop design. She has been working in the field of education for more than nine years.

- She has guided many students in career planning and other related areas like business writing, creating resumes, writing college essays, etc.

- As a trainer, she conducts workshops on communication skills, life skills management, spoken English, and grooming (manners & etiquette).

- She is associated with Maharashtra University of Health Sciences as a trainer where she is involved in training teachers and students in Education Technology, Communication Skills, and Business Communication.

- She works as an independent career advisor & trainer at her firm En Route Career Advisor (www.enroutecareeradvisor.com) in Pune, Maharashtra.